We Are The Kitties

Read This Or I'll Bite You

INKBLOT BOOKS

We Are The Kitties
Read This Or I'll Bite You

Published by Inkblot Books
www.inkblotbooks.com
ISBN 1-932461-13-2

Cover image © 2006 Katrina Lovett

Published in the United States of America

Kitties Of The Blogosphere

~Table Of Contents~

Foreword from The Psychokitty

When I began blogging in 2003, the blogosphere was a very lonely place for a kitty to play. While I mused about the odd habits of my People, and their abuse via the withholding of Stinky goodness and crunchy treats on demand, and the chronic exposure of my beautiful self to the neighborhood Sticky Little People, I also surfed the Internets looking for other cats who were opening their minds and hearts to the world.

It was lonely. I felt as if I were adrift on a sea of fleshy, furless creatures with no appreciation for feline angst. For over a year I poured my soul onto virtual paper, with only Humans to interact with, and while I felt I provided a much needed voice of reason in the din of whine, I longed for others such as myself. Cats with Internet access, and no fear of venturing forth in the blogosphere.

And then it happened. I found Timothy Dickens. And then Prince Muddy Paws. And Oreo. And William of Mass Destruction. It was as if a secret door had finally been opened, and all the other kitties were allowed in to play with me. There are now hundreds of cats with blogs, and the Net is no longer a lonely place for a kitty to play.

We're a sea of kitties of all colors, shapes, sizes, and breeds. There are happy ginger kitties and snarky tuxedo kitties. There are hysterically funny Meezers and Manxes. There are several joyful, thoughtful and kind kitties. What was once a lonely place is now a tremendous feline community.

And we like to share. Well, perhaps not with our feline siblings, but with other kitties in general. All agreed that whatever profits are derived from this collection of essays, stories, and poetry would be donated to other kitties in need. It bites, but reality is that there are kitties without forever homes, without enough food to get through the days, and without someone who loves them for just being their furry little selves.

We are the kitties of the blogosphere; we might bite, but we mean well.

~Max, January 2007

EVIL, OHIO
Max the PsychoKitty

Once upon a time there was an Evil Place called Ohio, and it was populated with Evil People. They were Evil, the Woman says, because they would get up at Way Too Early in the morning to do horrible things, such as Walking and Aerobics Class, and they would force her into getting up and doing them, too.

Oh, and it was Evil for other things, too. Like snow. The snow was cold and wet, and made my People say Bad Things and kept them inside for days at a time, where they tormented me endlessly with their talking and watching TV and their breathing. I dreaded the Days of Snow, simply because I knew I would not have the endless hours of peace and quiet to which I am rightly entitled.

Let's face it: the home is the cat's domain. The People are there to serve the cat, and when the cat does not wish to be served, the People should either Be Quiet or Not Be Home. But on those snow days, the People were home, making all kinds of senseless noise, cooking food that they refused to share with me, trying to pet me and play with me and make me curl up on their laps.

They blamed the snow on being in Ohio, which only makes me believe in its inherent Evilness all the more.

In this Evil Place, there were Sticky Little People. I could see them from my window, playing outside when it was warm, running and screaming and throwing things at each other. They played in the dirt near the window, digging and scratching their way through the earth as if they expected to find some sort of treasure, or live wiggling worms with which they could torment their parents.

Day after day they were out there, and the People would sit in chairs on the grass, watching them. Often, the female People would bring out food and feed the Sticky Little People, and sometimes themselves. The older of the Sticky People were capable of getting the food from their plates into their own mouths, but the smaller of them needed assistance, and so the People would stop what they were doing—which was usually just endless talk about Nothing in Particular as far as I could tell—to spoon food into those eager little mouth, or to break off small bites of whatever they were having to give to the little ones.

Deep down, I knew that these small people were danger wrapped in tiny shoes and oversized shorts and t-shirts. If they could, they would reach through the window and grab my fur or my tail, tugging and pulling until I screamed, or until my tail came loose in a giant bloody mess. I watched them through the safety of the window, paying close attention to their every move.

I even learned their names. Jacob, Mercedes, Patrick, Sammi, Jonathan, Stephanie, Kimberly, Matthew, and Rhiannon.

These were the spawn of the Evil People.

These creatures were those whom I must avoid in the flesh at all costs, lest my fur be rendered from my beautiful frame. Or, at the very least, lest I be swept up into a tight, sticky, peanut butter laden hug.

There were other Sticky Little People, but they came and went, as Sticky Little People are wont to do. Those nine, they were the most persistent. They played outside my window with amazing regularity, and the Evil from which they spewed forth stayed sometimes until well after dark, when the Sticky Little People were in their beds and asleep.

They stayed there in their plastic chairs on the grass, drinking Red Drinks (which only made them more loud and more stupid) listening through monitoring devices for the sounds of their slumbering offspring. They talked and laughed, and exposed my People to such levels of Evil that I wasn't sure I could comprehend it all.

The snow days, as much as I hated them, provided at least some barrier between my People and the Evil Ones. When there was snow, no one played in the yard, and no one stayed there until after dark, drinking Red Stupid Drinks and engaging in the exposure of evilness.

I suffered through two seasons of snow days, which meant I also suffered through two seasons of Days Nice Enough To Engage In Evil. In the mornings the Woman dragged herself out of bed, lest the Evil People break down the door and bodily carry her outside to do all the walking and aerobicizing, and in the afternoons she was outside watching the Sticky Little People play, talking to their female parents, sometimes to the occasional male parent who happened to be there.

I suffered through those seasons, knowing something Really Bad had to come of it. It was not possible for the People to be exposed to so much Evil without it seeping in through their pitiful, furless flesh. The Bad Thing was coming, and I could feel it.

And came it did.

It came in small steps. First, the People put me inside the Plastic Tomb which was brought to the house by the Evil delivery man in his Evil brown truck. The Woman wanted me to like it; it was blue plastic that I could see through, with wide slots to allow air inside, and a pad upon which she expected me to curl up and nap, as if I had nary an active cell inside my brain. She placed this tomb upon the floor with the door open, inviting me to investigate, to crawl inside and be comfortable. And when I did, when curiosity got the better of me, she closed the door.

She took me outside.

Outside, where the Evil People sat in their semicircle of Red Stupid drinks, where the Sticky Little People could reach through the slots with their sticky little fingers to touch me. Oh, the Evil Ones all told their spawn to "be soft" and "quiet, don't scare him" but I knew they only wanted me terrified and angry.

I was not about to become what they wished, so I leaned my head forward and sniffed the fingers of the youngest of the Sticky People. He squealed as if delighted, and withdrew his fingers, knowing I might decide to bite one off.

Then another Sticky Person approached. She did

not stick her fingers in to touch me; she squatted before me and smiled, and squeezing words from around the pacifier wedged happily between her lips, said "Math!"

"Yes," the Evil People laughed, "that's Max!"

They played a game of the Evilness, trying to make it appear as though this was All Good Fun. But I knew better. This was the Evil In Training; first get the Woman to bring me out, a small step in her recruitment to their dark ways.

Next, she placed a small table near the front door, so that I could see outside through the screen door, and sniff the fresh air. Sticky Little People would come up to me, their fingers resting on the mesh as they giggled and called me Math. Jacob the Blond would stand there and say "Hi!" before he crouched out of sight. When I was sure he was gone he would pop back up and laugh, and say "Hi" again.

"He's playing peek-a-boo with you, Max," the Woman said. "He likes you."

The feeling, I assured her, driving the point home by leaning back, hiking my leg up, and licking myself, was not mutual.

Still, I couldn't help myself. I had to keep looking out the door. It was better than the window; at the door I could smell their intentions as much as I could smell the sourness of their sippy cups filled with milk. I learned their games of hide and seek, and I accepted that they could poke the screen and talk to me without grabbing my fur.

I relaxed. I made the mistake of relaxing in the presence of the Sticky Little People.

It was then that the Evilness began to expand exponentially. The People became nervous and tired, and the air was filled with Something Is Happening. I could sense it, but I was distracted by the Sticky Little People, and did not give it my full consideration.

Then one day the Woman scooped me up and locked me in the bathroom. I was alone in there with only my litterbox, some dry crunchy food, and a water dish. Oh, and a bed. She gave me a bed upon which I could wait, wondering at the sounds I was hearing through the door, dull footsteps that approached and retreated, strange voices that were muddled and tired.

She was outside, I was sure of it, outside with the Evil Ones, watching those Sticky Little People play. And she forgot me, I know she forgot me, because it was hours later before she let me out.

When she did, the house was filled with boxes. Every room was jammed full of them, and the smell of old cardboard invaded my senses. Still she sat outside with the Evil People, as they ate food and sucked down drink after drink after Stupid Drink.

Oh, and it got worse.

Two days later she scooped me up and threw me into the bathroom again, and from there I listened to new strange voices, and new odd footsteps. She was outside again, basking in the sunshine as I curled up not three feet from my litterbox. I laid there and I cursed my People for their inconsideration, and wondered how many more boxes there would be once I was finally let out from my makeshift jail.

A dozen? Two dozen? More?

I waited and dozed, knowing here was not much I could do. When I heard the familiar steps of her oversized shoes coming towards the door I sat up and took a deep breath, because it might be the last clean breath I had for a while. Those boxes are, after all, voraciously stinky.

She opened the door and I stomped out, determined to demonstrate every level of indignity I felt. I was going to give her a piece of my mind, let her know in no uncertain terms—

—but there were no boxes. There wasn't anything. Every single thing we owned was gone.

We were robbed!

As I was trapped inside that little bathroom, as she lounged out in the sun with her Evil friends, someone snuck into the house and took every single thing we had. Oh, there were a few things left, like a couple of blankets and a blow up mattress, but the important things were gone.

The Supreme Commander Kitty Tower, which had been so close to the table that I could pounce during their meals was gone.

My window perches, from which I could view the world were gone.

The big comfy chair in the living room was gone.

It was all gone, and she didn't seem the least bit concerned about it. She blew up a mattress and spent the evening curled up there, trying to make me feel better, but deep down I knew this was the work of Evil.

She LET someone come in and take all our stuff.

Over the next few days she cleaned the empty house, as if cleaning made up for the lack of anything fun to do. The cleaning was peppered by moments of sitting outside, where I was taken in my blue Plastic Tomb, where the Sticky Little People could annoy me with their little fingers poking at me through the slots, and where they could pound on the plastic in spite of parental protests.

It was there, in the front yard amongst the Evil Ones and their spawn, that I felt the first real stirrings of Evil emanating from my People. I knew, without a doubt, that they had passed their apprenticeship and were becoming Truly Evil themselves. Something was happening, and I could feel it coming to me on the breeze that drifted in through the slats of my plastic tomb.

I slept fitfully that night, knowing The Big Bad was coming.

And the next morning, they shoved me into the plastic tomb and then shoved that tomb into the back seat of their car. I began voicing my displeasure, but they paid no attention. They simply stood in the yard with the Evil People, looking rather sad and a bit uncomfortable, and after some time they hugged the Evil Ones and then got in the car with me.

"I want to go home," I told them as they drove away. "Let me out and let me go home!"

They kept telling me everything was going to be all right, but I knew better. It didn't *feel* all right, it felt awkward and weird and EVIL.

They kept me in that tomb all day long. Mile after mile of the road rumbling beneath me; I voiced my displeasure for hours, hoping they would turn around and take me home. They would not buckle; at one point the Woman turned around and looked at me and said "I'm starting to understand shaken baby syndrome as it applies to kitties."

That did not shut me up.

I howled. I meowed. I mehowled. I wanted out, I wanted home, and I was making sure they knew it.

They stopped once in a while, but they did not let me out. A few times during the day they offered me treats, and even bits of chicken they took from some guy they called The Colonel. (I hope he wasn't too upset that they took it, but his chicken was rather tasty.) But it wasn't until dark when they reached into the car and un-strapped the tomb from its many restraints.

"Are we home?" I asked hopefully, but no, we were in a strange place, a single room with strange beds and odd smells of Other Peoples' gaseous anomalies and odd funk.

I did not want to live in that room, but if I had to, I was sure I could make the best of it.

But the next morning, it started anew. And every morning thereafter, for four mornings, it was the same: grab the kitty and force him into the plastic tomb. Drive until everyone is numb and cranky. Sleep in a strange room.

But then on the 4th day, something wonderful happened. We stopped early and went into yet another strange room, and the People said, take it easy, Max, it's almost over.

I pondered what "almost" meant, when there was a knock at the door. It was the Younger Human and his Much Better Smelling Friend! The People had taken me back to my Younger Human! He was the one who brought me home first, the one who had saved me from life without certainty.

Ok, at that moment my life wasn't exactly filled with certainty since I had no idea where I was or even what day it was, but he brought me from a place I'd mostly forgotten but knew I wanted to forget, to the People, who were mostly all right until they started hanging around Evil.

And the Evil wasn't so bad until it led to four days in a car, trapped there with the People and their ever increasing funk that even a hot shower could not erase.

I was shy around the Younger Human, but I was glad to see him. He smelled like home, something I wasn't sure I would ever smell again. And then he went away, but they said I would see him again and soon.

And the next morning, they did not stuff me into a plastic tomb. They told me to stay put and to rest while they went out and found a new place to live, someplace I would be happy.

Later on they came back and said they found a place, and the next morning they put me in the tomb, but the Woman promised it was only for 5 minutes. And she kept her promise; after 5 minutes I was in another strange new place, one without someone else's beds and pillows and disturbing foul odors.

I spent the rest of the day slinking around the strange new place, listening to my meows echo off the walls. It was empty, except for the things they had brought with them in the car, but they assured me it was home.

A week later I was locked in the bathroom again. I pondered the meaning of it all: we had nothing left, how could anyone come in and take all our stuff? And where was the Woman? She didn't have a front yard filled with Sticky Little People and the Evil Ones to distract her. There was this sliver of space they called the Patio, but it really wasn't big enough to sit out there, and there were certainly no Evil Ones with whom she could occupy time. And no Stupid Red Drinks.

About the time I had decided that maybe this was MY home and not theirs, she opened the door. A flood of fresh air washed over me, and as I walked out of the bathroom I realized the room was filled with boxes. And so was the next room. And the room after that. And there was my Supreme Commander Kitty Tower.

Away from Ohio, and the influences of Evil, our belongings were finally located and returned. The People emptied them from the boxes, assembled them in some sort of logical order, and proclaimed we were finally Home. Life as I knew it would go on.

Well, until they brought another cat home, and it was sick, and it got me sick and I nearly DIED.

And until they decided we needed a bigger place to live.

And until they had to move AGAIN.

In this new new place, I have windows like I did in Ohio. I can see everything going on outside, but the Woman does not sit out front with anyone, and there are no Sticky Little People to observe in the midst of their play.

No one has called me "Math" in so long that I barely remember it happening.

I see no Evil, I hear no Evil.

But really, I kind of miss the Evil. As the new kitty, who is no longer so new and is appropriately named Buddah Pest, sneaks up and bites my tail yet again, I wonder where the all the Sticky Little People are. And if

they're still little. And if they remember playing pee-a-
boo with me through the screen door, and being told be
to soft with me.

> This is my life now, lacking Evil.
> But I don't miss it, oh no.
> No.
> No.
> No.

Feline Love

My love is endless, forever.
It knows no bounds,
holds no grudges.
I have forgotten everything you have done,
late food, late water, no warm lap
when I need one, sometimes.
Because you chose me,
made a home for me,
forgive me,
talk to me, pet me,
and love me back.
All this in a purrrrr.

~brandi

A Day In The Life Of
Icat Skeeterovitch
Skeeter

Midnight - Wake up. Stretch. Sniff nose of The Big Thing to see if he is awake. He isn't. Sneeze on his face to wake him up. Ah, get scratched for 10 whole minutes. Purr.

00:10 - Walk away in mid-purr. Go sniff "crunchies" bowl. Eat a couple crunchies as loudly as possible in case The Big Thing has fallen asleep already. Stare out the hard clear thing for a while.

00:30 - Use litterbox. Wander around basement a while.

01:00 - Go upstairs. See "flappy-moth-thing" outside the hard clear thing. Bat at it for a while until it goes away. Sleep on the mat by the hard clear thing.

02:00 - Wake up. Stretch. Go find LC to see if she wants to play. She doesn't. She's warm and nappy. I poke at her a few times, she yawns, and turns her back on me. Go sit on the table for a while, since The Big Thing isn't up to shoo me off.

02:10 - Sleep on table.

04:00 - Wake up. LC is nudging me. She wants to play. We play "hot-paws" for a while and then get down to some serious wrassling.

04:10 – The Big Thing gets up and tells us to stop making so much noise. We stare at him and then curl up together so he knows we aren't really fighting.

05:00 – Strange animal outside the hard clear thing! LC and I both study it for a while and then decide we want it to go away. We both growl at it.

05:10 – The Big Thing gets up to see what the problem is. "It's just a possum", he says. But he watches it with us for a few minutes until it wanders away. He makes sure there are crunchies in our bowl, goes back to the warm softy thing, and falls asleep again.

06:00 – The light starts outside. I want to go OUT! I go nudge The Big Thing, but he just won't respond. I go use the litterbox again (hey, why isn't it clean?). I use the second one. LC is waiting to use it, too, so I sit next to it a while. She has to wait because she hates it when I watch.

06:05 – Get bored and go upstairs. Drink water. Find the soft thing on the closet floor and sleep on it.

08:00 - Wake up. The Big Thing is doing his sprayed water bath. He must be Unsane! Go back to sleep.

08:30 – The Big Thing has put on his fur and is walking around. Maybe I can get OUT! I walk to the hard clear thing and say very distinctly "me-out". Instead, he grabs me and squirts some pink cold "med-i-ca-shun" in my mouth. I squirm and twist, but I can't avoid it. I don't know why he thinks I like this stuff, but at least I get some real wet good food afterwards.

08:35 – LC comes to the food bowl and he grabs her. She gets the same cold pink stuff, and a small bowl of her own.

09:00 – The Big Thing is moving stuff around. I watch carefully to make sure he doesn't step on me. He very seldom does, but you never know.

10:00 – The Big Thing opens the hard clear thing and I sit there with my head OUT smelling the air! LC is pacing behind me trying to get out. She never wants to check things first.

10:01 – LC finally jumps over me to get OUT.

10:05 - Nothing pounces LC, so I go out too. LC is off the deck already, but I go sit under the table and watch the world for a while. And I watch carefully to make sure The Big Thing isn't going to close the hard clear thing before I can run back inside.

10:15 – Go into the yard. Find a good place to pee.

10:16 – Find a good place to poop.

10:17 – Wander around the yard. LC is staring at The Wall. She's going to jump it, I just know. I don't understand why she does that. It is scary outside The Wall. Doggies and Strange Big Things and Noisy Metal Things, oh my!

10:20 – LC is sitting on top of The Wall. The Big Thing calls to LC to get down from there. She does. On the Other Side. She's Unsane!

10:30 – The Big Thing is picking up tree-pieces. Collecting them in piles. I watch from a distance. He drags pawfuls of tree-pieces from around the yard to the place where he goes through The Wall. Then he goes back inside.

10:45 – It's lonely with LC outside The Wall and The Big Thing inside the cave. The air is cool and the bright thing is warm. I take a nap under the close little-trees.

11:30 – LC is back. I sniff her thoroughly to see what she has been doing. We lick each other's heads.

Then she walks away and I sniff where she was sitting. I like that!

11:35 – LC found a froggie and brought it to the grassy area. I sniff it, but I don't smell anything warm, so I walk away. She eats it. Yuck and Why? It's just all cold…

11:40 – LC is eating, so I want something to eat. I go off to the places where the mousies are and settle down to listen.

12:00 – A rustle! I twitch my ears around to find the source and I wait.

12:05 – And wait

12:10 – And wait.

12:15 – Nothing any more. I go and sniff the place where the sound came from. Just a hole with no mousie. It didn't come out! But it almost did; it was at least, there.

12:16 – Go back on the deck under the table to watch across The Wall. Sleep. The Big Thing closed the hard clear thing while I wasn't looking.

13:00 – The hard clear thing opens! I run back inside. I'm hungry! Crunchies!

13:05 – Since The Big Thing is off the warm softy thing, I sleep on it.

We Are The Kitties!

13:30 – LC comes and curls up next to me. I lick her head a few times and we both sleep.

15:00 - The Big Thing has turned on the sparkly-box, and made a tired groaning sound. That means he is sitting. I get up, stretch, and walk out to him. Sure enough, there is a LAP! I hop up and get scratched for a while.

15:10 – I curl up and sleep. Warm. Safe. Kitty-dreams of mommy-cat. I purr. The Big Thing purrs (in his own way).

15:30 – I get jostled a bit. The Big Thing is about to stand up. I stare at him a lick, yawn, and stretch. Then he helps be down to the floor of the cave. I go look out the hard clear thing a while.

15:50 – LC wakes up and wants to play. We wrassle a bit. The Big Thing just smiles. Why is it OK to wrassle when he watches but not OK to wrassle when he is sleeping?

15:55 – LC bites my ear and I get mad and hit her. She walks away. I sniff the place where she was sitting.

16:00 – I go to drink some water from the bubbly thing. LC is already there, so I have to wait.

16:05 – Still waiting. LC thinks the bubbly thing is a toy. She waits for the bubbles to come and then tries to catch them. But they are inside and she can't. Doesn't she know that? But maybe that is like the flappy-moth-things. We can pretend.

16:10 – LC gives up and walks away from the bubbly thing. It's my turn. I drink and get the bubbles! LC runs over to watch them. I run away. I don't like those kinds of surprises like she does. And I don't like it when LC runs at me. She likes to knock me over.

16:15 – The Big Thing is outside again, but he has the opening in The Wall open, so the hard clear thing is closed and we can't go outside. He is dragging those pawfuls of tree-stuff through it. He must have the Place We Cannot Go full of that stuff because he seems to do that lots.

17:00 – The Big Thing is back inside. He smells like trees, and he has little sticky seeds all over him. He always pulls those off of us, so when he sits down in front of the sparkly-box again, I start licking him. I get a few off, and he starts picking them off himself too. Must stay clean!

17:05 – As he is doing a better job at removing the stickies, I just curl up on his lap. He even fids a few on me and removes them. Purr!

17:10 Hey, it's past dinnertime! I stand up ad sniff his face and tell him. He looks at me a lick and then at a thing on his paw, and laughs. He gets up and goes to the wet good stuff place. I see the little can in his hand and dance all around him.

17:11 – What? He grabbed me again and squirted that pink cold stuff down my throat! ACK! I run away as soon as he releases me. That was mean...

17:15 – From under the bed, I smell the wet good stuff, so I cautiously come out. LC is already eating her part, so I run over to make sure she doesn't eat mine, too. In fact, I decide I like her bowl better, so I shove my head in. She backs away, like always (well, I'm a lot bigger than she is, so I get to choose). She goes over to the other bowl.

17:30 – We get to go outside again! LC runs over to the pond to look for fishies and froggies. I sit on the deck under the table and the last light. Watching over The Wall for threats, of course. There are some little Big Things out there, but they are not making much noise, so I stay out. I wonder when The Big Thing feeds them? I never see him do it.

17:31 – Maybe they feed themselves. The Big Thing is the source of all food (but froggies and mousies we catch on our own) and he must give the other Big Things their food too. Or do they get food on their own? They seem to have their own caves, too. Ooh, my head hurts...

17:32 – Sleep.

18:00 – The Big Thing opened the hard clear thing, and we can come back inside. LC was already there waiting. I stuck my head in and LC jumped over me. We both went and ate the rest of the wet good food.

18:30 – Litterbox time. They're clean. I use one and LC uses the other (I didn't stare). The Big Thing is down there too, and he comes over when we are done with "our business". He opens the wall to the strange room we can seldom go. That's where he keeps the Big Noisy Metal Thing. But it isn't making any noise now, so we both go in to sniff around. There are lots of interesting smells there. Sometimes fishies and sometimes meat.

18:45 – We are done sniffing the strange room and back inside. The Big Thing opens the hard clear thing. LC goes out, but I stay inside with my nose out. It is windyish and I don't like that. I go to other opening-places and demand to see what it is like out those places, but it is windyish in all of them. I decide to stay in.

19:00 – The Big Thing has given food to himself and it smells great. But we know we are not allowed to be near his own food bowl, so we stay on the floor of the cave while he eats. He is quite firm about that. But sometimes he gives us a little piece from his food bowl. We're NOT begging (begging is wrong), but asking is OK. I like his chickie food better than most things he eats (and he eats plants - Yuck!). And if you aren't there, you can't get any.

19:30 – The Big Thing has finished eating, and is spreading some paper across the table. It is OK for us to come up on that. He pays us a lot of attention whenever we sit where he is looking. He scratches us, at least, and sometimes moves our tail around. Sometimes he even picks us up and puts us back down in another favored place on his paper.

20:00 – Time to nap. LC is already on the warm softy thing, so I join her. I give her a few head licks and then sleep. She is warm, I am warm, we are warm. The Big Thing is quiet.

21:00 – The Big Thing is in the next part of the Cave. That's where he sits and taps stuff in front of the small sparkly box. It isn't so sparkly, but we sometimes see other kitties (and shapes) on it. I like to go sit under the thing he sits on.

21:10 – I'm all wrapped around the bottom of the thing The Big Thing sits on in front of the small sparkly box. There are hard things around the bottom, but they are a good place for my head to rest. I wish he would cover it with blankies, though!

21:45 - The Big Thing has been going tap-tap-tap above me. It must be a great toy. I tried it once, and he got upset, though, so I guess it is just his toy. I understand that. LC has her toys and I have mine.

22:00 – The Big Thing is done playing with his toy. So I have to be careful. Once, he shoved the sitty-thing back to get up and I got my tail hurt! So I look up and he looks down. If I am there, he tells me he is going to move the sitty-thing. I usually move. If I don't, he moves me for myself.

22:05 – Treat time! I got some soft ones I like and LC got some hard ones she likes. I'll eat hers, but she doesn't like mine. So The Big Thing sits on the floor of the cave between us and hands us what we like best.

22:30 – Sleep time again. I sleep under the big softy thing (it's so protective-feeling) and LC sleeps on the top (it's warmer). The Big Thing joins us (LC has to move for a moment). Sometimes I join them on top and even crawl under the blankie thing. I get scratched lots that way, but it gets too warm after a while, and I go back under the big softy thing.

Midnight - Wake up. Stretch. Sniff nose of The Big Thing to see if he is awake. He isn't. Sneeze on his face to wake him up. Ah, get scratched for 10 whole minutes. Purr.

Tilli's Snow Adventure
A madeup story by Jessica and Tilli.

Tilli sat at the window, looking out at the white swirly stuff that was slowly coating the pebbled garden. Eager to escape into this cool new stuff, Tilli leapt lightly to to wooden floor and started call for her people.

Fast steps indicated that Jessica was first on the scene. "No, Tilli!" She said, scooping the little cat into her arms. "WHY NOT!?" Mewed Tilli angrily. "no!" Jessica said, sarcastically, clearly not understanding.

"Thicko…" Tilli muttered, leaping from her arms. "LET ME OUT! LET ME OUT!" She began to cry. With a sigh, Jessica returned to surfing the net in the loft. Next on the scene was the mother human. Tilli mewed "YAY!" As the door was opened. Rushed footsteps indicated Jessica's rush into the room to stop Tilli getting out.

"Mew!" Tilli leapt out, onto the cold flakes. "Cold!" She cried, immediately leaping back in. Jessica laughed at her and Tilli flicked her tail irritably. "That's snow, Tilli!" Jessica laughed, watching the irritable cat. Tilli leapt lightly out again.

As soon as Tilli's paws adjusted to the cold, she began to leap after the dancing snow flakes. But from then on, she prefered to sit on the windowsill instead of leap after the cold, dancing flakes!

The End.

Outside.

She runs out,
into the sunlight.
new things out here!
she sniffs,
then looks at the tree.
Too high for me!

A few months later.
She runs out.
leaps.
up into the tree.
peeking from the branches.
She's outside!
Up the Tree!

~Jessica & Tilli

Cheryl Pierce & The Gang Of Four

Reveille

In darkness she rises,
Blindly totters kitchenward,
Trusting. Barefoot.
squish Oh, gawd!
Mousepart? Hairball?
Bile and wrath rise equally!
—*Edmund Hillary Pierce, aka Sir*
Edmund the Rotund

Nelson John LaPurr

I'm slinky and sneaky, a sleek, naughty cat.
My black tail, black spot, and saucy black cap
Can be glimpsed near the site of crimes galore:
Spilled beads, torn books, and pens on the floor.

I commit planticide with the greatest of ease,
And my glare brings the other cats to their knees.

If there's a place a cat shouldn't be seen
It's sure that LaPurr will soon make the scene.

In repose, I am haughty. My basilisk stare
Can chill you right through. You know you don't dare
Cross *this* kitty or ruffle his fur—
I'm Nelson the Wicked—N. J. LaPurr!

—*Nelson J. L. Pierce*

Wouldn't YOU like to know!
(or, Is There an Oneiromancer in the House?)

Cat sleeps.
Cat dreams.
Cat smiles.
Cat schemes?
Time tells.

—*Nitro Pierce*

Xing Song

I'm cuddlesome and green-eyed,
But I whisper in your brain:
"Death to those who'd touch my toes,
my keen claws to profane.
All you'll hear is 'whicker-snick',
then fall among the slain."

— *Xing Lu Pierce*

Lionettes

Deep tawny gold, ears brushed with black,
Stealthy on their victims' track,

We Are The Kitties!

A leap, a pounce, a fleeting tussle—
A struggle won with spring-steel muscle.

Jungle cats of might and brawn
Aren't often found on green, groomed lawn;
So how can I describe these frays?
At home I see them every day.

Tiny hunters stalk my halls,
Tumbling toys, rolling yarn balls.
Sometimes the tail's the only way
To tell what's kitten and what's prey!

        — Cheryl C. Pierce

Charlie

Charles (the fluffy-tailed Balinese)
Is liquid-boned, languid, and easy to please.
This quiet cat has arctic-blue eyes
And an off-center stare that can hypnotize.

His fur is pale cream tipped with soft grey,
And it shimmers with light like a new-born day.
How splendid his whiskers! How dainty his paws;
He pats you so gently, never uses his claws.

He's trusting and docile, just a little bit shy.
All taken together, a loveable guy
Who doesn't ask much (just a chin-rub or two)
And some of his nap times taken on you!

        — Cheryl C. Pierce

Prrrrrow, the Literary Cat

He announced himself at the door one day,
A Russian Blue in looks.
Who knew, when we let him in to stay,
He'd develop a taste for books?

I don't mean he was a critic,
Perusing them and sitting back
To meditate about an ethic
Or ruminate on what they lacked.

Oh no; his interest was digestive!
He was a scholarly gourmand
Who dined on print, sober or festive,
From whatever text was at hand.

No book was safe with him around—
He'd nibble corners, lick the pages—
Both paperbacks and leather-bound.
He'd relish them, eat them by stages!

Absorbing knowledge, art, or fashion
(T'was all the same to him)
Became an all-consuming passion;
He devoured books both thick and thin.

But when he wasn't munching paper,
He'd lounge about and just look wise.
Did he retain what he had savored?
Was he a bookworm in disguise?

— *Cheryl C. Pierce*

Amos, Son of Genghis
Charles B. Cree, IV

Amos and the Kamikaze Kat

Two a.m. and the screams echoed around the city block. The struggle was brief but fierce. The morning sun revealed much about the titanic struggle—footprints in the light dust, shreds of white Angora fur. Something had to be done.

Amos stretched lazily. There was no sign of injury, not a new one anyway. The long, meandering scar across his broad nose and the missing wedge-shaped chunk, obviously bitten out, at the top of his ear, bespoke previous battles. His thick neck and muscular face hinted that he usually was the victor, but he was no longer young. If he planned to hold onto his territory and live long enough to enjoy it, he needed to be smarter about how he did it. The years had snuck up on him. Was he too old and decrepit to continue with a reasonable expectation of success? How old was Amos? For an apple, he was very old. For a tree, he was very young. For a cat, he was just right. Yes, a cat, but not just any cat. At age seven, Amos was big, tough, and just a bit grumpy. Play time was over. It was time for business—cruising the neighbor-hood, asserting his presence, protecting his domain.

His courage was never in doubt. Amos was the only cat I've ever known who feared nothing—not cats, not dogs, not raccoons, and certainly not mere humans. Most of Amos's psyche was filled with mean, leaving precious little area left for fear. However, there are old warriors and there are bold warriors; but there are no old, bold warriors. Amos needed a better strategy.

The keeper of the white Angora had grown tired of the repeated vet visits. Kamikaze Kat was now tethered to the cherry tree across the street and unable to invade Amos's territory, but that made no difference. Amos set out to teach Kamikaze Kat one final lesson about exactly who was in charge. This would take some consideration.

One morning Amos strolled across the street into the Angora's territory. His approach was deliberate and without stealth. The big white fuzzball eagerly watched him coming all the way. Could his luck be changing? Could he now scrap with Amos on his own turf? His charge was cut short by the tether, and Amos casually sat just a foot from the now screaming, foaming cat. While Amos calmly ignored the frenetic Kamikaze, he examined the tree and the rope with supreme interest. Cats can't count, measure, or calculate; but they can compare. His gaze went to the tree, then to the rope, then back to the tree at least a dozen times. Satisfied with his ruminations, he turned toward home and ambled across the street.

Amos's routine did not vary. He marched in the back door with some gruff language, sauntered through the living room, and at the right time, went out the front door for some meditation on the porch railing. He may have cast a glance toward his ultimate target from the comfort of the rail, but I never saw it. When the angle of the sun told him it was time for business, across the street he went. He used that same slow, rolling gait and never hurried or skulked. The Angora didn't miss his approach and rose to a hissy fit each time. Settling onto the same spot as the day before, Amos watched—first the rope, then the tree; then he came home. Just what was his agenda? There was something going on in that big round head, but what?

Day four: oh, I had to watch. There seemed to be something new in Amos's gait, something subtle and confident. Something had to break. Cats look patient, but they have a short attention span. The Angora saw him coming early and couldn't wait to begin the histrionics; but Amos was unmoved. With that low, rolling gait by which he could be identified from a block away, Amos calmly crossed the street and found his accustomed spot, 20 feet out from the base of the tree. There he sat, alternating his gaze between Kamikaze Kat and the branches of the cherry tree. Now the Angora, now the branches. Up and down. Back and forth. What was he looking at? What was he considering? His scrutiny of the Angora's condition was more than idle curiosity, and in less time than it takes to describe, we knew why.

In a movement without warning, Amos leapt into full stride, passed the startled Kat, and ascended the cherry tree. Literally running up the trunk, he sprinted up a limb, and pussyfooted (yeah, yeah, I know) into the branches at the top of the tree. Reacting instantaneously, the Angora was in pursuit—up the trunk, out a limb, and into the branches with a grace unique to felines. Amos leapt from the topmost branches, cutting a graceful arc that belied his age. He catapulted himself outward and then downward, toward his original spot on the ground. The Angora followed Amos's exact route, creating a fine shower of leaves and bark in pursuit of his aging prey. The blood lust was upon him and he would not be denied. He was closing the gap and it was just a matter of time; or was it? By the time Amos hit the ground very near his original launch point, the Angora was airborne with all his eggs in one irreversible basket.

But Amos didn't continue his escape. Instead he sat back down in his favorite vantage point, waiting, watching, and calculating as he had done for the previous three days. "Yeowwwww!" The battle cry was cut short by the slack coming out of the tether, now threaded through the limbs and branches of the cherry tree, and Kamikaze Kat's descent was cut short by about four feet. He yowled and hissed until gravity and his noose robbed him of the ability to vocalize. There he dangled, while Amos sat, calmly relishing the Angora's predicament.

"Oh my." I sprang for the phone and, as speed dial was several decades away, I struggled with dialing the seven digits that would bring me in contact with the owner. "Mrs. Tarbell, your cat is committing suicide," I blathered into the phone. "What? Who is this? What are you talking about?" Yeah, right, how much of this is making sense?

"Your cat is strangling in the back yard." A hand swept back the kitchen curtains; and the largest eyes I've ever seen caught a glimpse of Kamikaze Kat dangling at the end of 20 feet of clothesline, anchored to the base of the dwarf cherry tree.

With a sound best described as a St. Lawrence war whoop, the phone went dead Mrs. Tarbell bounded to the rescue of her beloved pet.

Amos seemed unexcited, unmoved, and unconcerned. Kamikaze Kat was never the same.

Amos and the Alsatian

Amos was unique as the only cat I've ever known who feared nothing. There must be a finite amount of space in a cat's psyche, and most of Amos's was occupied with … mean, leaving precious little area for fear.

He had developed a certain routine that, if left uninterrupted, he followed with great precision. At the back door, at the same hour every day, he'd 'vocalize' his presence. I was always grateful that a Human-Cat translator had not been invented, because Amos would've fried the circuits. Anyway, at the appointed hour, he would yeowl for access to the kitchen, where he'd yeowl for his breakfast. At the same time, he warned the other eight felines that he was not to be disturbed; he was rarely interrupted. Then, having satisfied his hunger, Amos would stroll into the living room and assume his comfort on the back of the couch which, coincidentally, the sun had just begun to warm. As ol' Sol continued his traverse of the sky, casting a shadow on the 'throne', Amos would retire to the side porch, find another spot in the sunlight, and continue his ruminations on the railing. When the sun no longer warmed his ancient hide, it was time to move on and conduct night missions around the neighborhood.

Most of the time this routine came and went without a hitch, but today someone would disturb his pattern and pay for that egregious mistake. On a typical summer afternoon Amos displayed exactly how little concern he had for genuine hazards.

I was standing at the front door, taking in the July sunset and thinking "The tiger is the gentlest creature in the forest. Why? Because he can afford to be" when an Alsatian Shepherd crashed the party. He chased one of our cats up the street and onto the porch then lost sight of her when she slipped through the front door screen, which had been hinged for easy entry and exit. The befuddled dog came to a screeching halt just inches from the spot where Amos rested on the porch railing.

This dog had killed several local cats, had bitten women and young children, and was feared by most who knew him. He was one bad dog. He was, however, about to meet someone even "badder." Now, he was nose to nose with the personification of animal badness.

Ah, yes, the canine nose; such a magnificently sensitive organ. It was over in the time it took to catch a breath. Amos made only two movements: His ears went down, giving that bucket of a head an even rounder appearance; and the rather large right paw swung a hook surely the envy of any boxer. The very sharp, but not very clean talons caught the crease of the dog's nose just as the big canine tried to reverse course. The yelp, its pitch in direct proportion to the level of discomfort, should have broken glass as the Alsatian didn't spare a single toenail getting traction for retreat as he left with just a tad less tissue than when he arrived.

Amos never got up. After all, there were still a few moments of sunshine left and he meant to enjoy them. A short glance at, and a quick lick of the weapon responsible for the dog's retreat, and it was business as usual. The taste of victory, or hygiene? I vote for the former.

The Derby Haikus
Derby

A secret no more
An adoring Princess
The one Mia Bella.

Brach is my buddy
White and buff tigers are we
Soul twins in our hearts

Chick magnet am I
Never believed it could be
A special blessing

I am a pretty cat
There is no doubt of that fact
Wisdom in my eyes.

Ancient and Modern *Cats* *Compare Notes*
Fat Eric and Kate Dixon

I am Bastet, divine feline, publicly-acclaimed cat goddess.

I am Eric, divine feline, self-acclaimed cat god.

My domain is in the city of Bubastis, in the region of Lower Egypt, on the eastern side of the River Nile.

My domain is in the city of London, in the region of Southern England, on the northern side of the River Thames.

My residence is a spacious temple, in the centre of the city, in which my many priestesses worship me.

My residence is a 3-bedroomed house, in a suburban street, in which my two human servants worship me.

In my garden, there is a canal a hundred feet wide, a wall adorned with sculptures, and a grove of fair tall trees next to the sacred effigies.

In my garden, there is a small pond, a wooden fence adorned with honeysuckle, and a line of rose bushes next to the recycling bins.

To celebrate my presence, my priests play on pipes of lotus and my priestesses play on cymbals and tambourines.

To celebrate my presence, the male human plays his Steely Dan CDs and the female human sings songs from West End musicals.

As the living embodiment of the feline goddess, I am given golden jewellery to wear and encouraged to eat first from the plates of my priestesses.

As the living embodiment of the feline god, I am given a blue collar to wear and discouraged from sneaking leftovers from the plates of my human servants.

To provide me with amusement, I am given golden ornaments and ibis feathers to play with, and cedarwood boughs to scratch.

To provide me with amusement, I am given furry mice and feathered sticks to play with, and a wicker mouse from IKEA to scratch.

I sleep on cushions of the finest wool and linen, surrounded by priestesses who fan me when the day is warm.

I sleep on carpets, duvets, human laps and fleecy cat beds, surrounded by humans who laugh at me when I am snoring.

When my priestesses come to offer me sustenance, I

recline, blinking lazily, next to my bejewelled statue while they are preparing the choicest morsels of food to be found in all Egypt.

When my human servants come to offer me sustenance, I jump up and down, squeaking excitedly, next to the fridge while they are opening the most expensive pouches of cat food to be found in all the supermarkets.

When my priestess is grooming me and anointing me with perfumes, I purr gently and sometimes even allow her to stroke my sacred head.

When my human servant is combing me and trying to clip my claws, I purr deafeningly, give her fluffy headbutts, and insist on licking her fingers, her hair, the comb and the claw clippers.

When we have a feast at my residence, my priestesses drink of the wine of the grape and say prayers at my altar.

When we have a feast at my residence, my human servants drink of the wine of the grape and tell really bad jokes.

As a mighty huntress, I am revered for my ability to kill cobras.

As a mighty hunter, I am laughed at for my attempts to catch frogs.

I am the protector of the home, the guardian against snakes, the watcher over the household, the keeper of truth and the goddess of the rising sun.

I am the protector of the home, the guardian against Evil Intruder Kitties, the watcher over the treat cupboard, the keeper of the comfortable spot on the bed and the god of the early breakfast alarm call.

I am also known as Ubasti, Lady of Flame, Eye of Ra, Kore Artemis, Perfumed Protector and Female Devourer.

I am also known as Fluffy Boy, Sweetiepie, Floofy Tum, Cuddly Dumpling, Gorgeous Ginger and Greedy Guts.

When I leave this world and go to the afterlife, I know my earthly remains will sleep in my necropolis at Per-Bast, and my priestesses will forget me and come to pay homage to other living incarnations of the goddess.

When I leave this world and go to the Bridge, I know my earthly remains will sleep beneath my favourite bush, and my human servants will never forget me, although they may come to love other cats.

Purr...
Purr...

Four deep on the bed, surrounding Mom.
She can't move.
Who cares? We're happy.
                                                    ~Tiger Lily

The Counter
Buddah

When I was just a little kitty we had to move to a new house and I didn't want to because I barely remembered being brought home from the shelter and I was afraid that I would get lost in a new place and no would be able to find me there and then I was afraid that maybe I was the only one moving into the new house but my brother kitty Max, who everyone calls PsychoKitty, said he had moved more times than he would like and it was okay because the Mom and the Dad and the Other Dad were going to come with us, and they had promised we would like the new house because it had stairs we could run up and down on and Max had stairs once before and said they were the greatest thing ever, and we would also have windows to look out of and we'd be able to see more than bushes, which was the only thing we could see out the apartment windows so moving would be all right even though it meant that we'd get locked in the bathroom while the Mom and the Dad and the Other Dad took all our stuff out of the apartment to take it to the new house, but when we got out of the bathroom they would take us there, and he was right, that's exactly what they did they took us to the new house and it had stairs that we could run up and down and the floors downstairs we were wood so I could play with my mousies and they would go zooooom across the floor really fast plus I could run and then stop fast and slide a long way, and when I was done sliding I could run back up the stairs, which were as much fun as Max said they would be, except he liked to get me on the top stair and head butt me so that I would fall down the stairs, but since he was actually playing with me I didn't complain about it, I just had fun and enjoyed it until the Mom and the Dad and the other Dad were all mad because not even a year later we had to move AGAIN and I was afraid we would have to go back to the apartment where there were no stairs and no windows to see out of and no hard floor to slide on but Max said to relax, that they would think of us when they picked a new place to live and he was right again, they found another house with stairs and wood floors to slide on, only this house is better because if a kitty sits on the stairs in the middle of the night and meows it sounds REALLY loud so Max does that just about every night, he gets on the stairs and says meow, meow, meow, meow, meow, meow, meow, meow until someone wakes up and tells him to shut up, which I think is a little rude because he's just singing but he thinks it's funny and that's the reason he does it, so he can annoy the Mom and the Dad but the Other Dad doesn't seem to mind because he sleeps with his door closed which means we can't go in there and play at night, but we can go in and play right on top of the Mom which she doesn't seem to appreciate but Max says she doesn't mind it as much as she says she does because it gives her something to blog about and she likes being able to blog about us because we're so cute, so I keep trying to think of cute things to do for her so she has things she can talk about, and I think I'm doing a pretty good job and Max does his share, too, like sometimes he crawls on top of her when she's asleep and sticks his nose up into one of her nostrils which makes her wake up and she's all grossed out but it really is funny, and sometimes he butts her nose with his head but he's not really sure WHY he does that, just that it annoys her and makes her nose hurt but he doesn't mean to make her nose hurt he just wants to have some fun, just like me so I play fetch with my toy mousies when I can get one of them to throw it for me and then I run after it and grab it and bring it back over and over and over because that's what fetch is, it's running after something and bringing it back over and over and over until the person you're playing with says "all right, we've played long enough," and they stop even though I'd like t keep playing so I have to go find something else to do and sometimes I try to get Max to play with me but he has to be in the right mood to play and that doesn't happen very often, so is he won't play I have to think of things to do all by myself, like jumping up on the bookcases right by the stairs which get me to this place on the wall that's like a thingy for kitties to walk on, if it were people walking on it they would call it a catwalk which just seems silly to me because there aren't any cats waking on the thingies they call a catwalk, but I walk on this thing and can look down on the Mom and the Dad when they're watching TV or reading and most of the time they see me up there and they stop and say

"Well, hello, Buddah, are you having fun up there?" and I always says "Yes, I am, thank you," and the Mom tells me to walk back and forth a lot because then she doesn't have to worry about figuring out how to get up there and dust, so not only am I having fun but I'm useful, too, and then when I'm done being high on the wall thingy I jump down and I got eat some crunchy food and sometimes I take a nap on the big comfy chair in the living room or I go into the Mom's office and get on top of the climbing tower where I can look out the window, but if Max is on top of the big climbing tower I have to get on the little one, but that's all right because they both have a good view out the window where we can watch Sticky Little People or sometimes Sticky Big People which Max says are actually teenagers but they look pretty sticky to him, and we can see when the Other Dad gets home, which we like because soon after he gets home the Mom and the Dad and the Other Dad have dinner and if it's something that won't make flames shoot out our butts, if we're good kitties we get to have a bite, and then we can go play or take naps, and then later the Mom opens a can of Stinky Goodness for us to share and because Max is greedy with Stinky Goodness I eat mine on the counter and he eats his on the floor and that's the best thing about the new house, I get to eat on the counter and I never have to worry about Max stealing my Stinky Goodness, which he did in the other house, and that's a good thing to like about having to move, never having to share your Stinky Goodness.

Owned by Five
Dee Francis

I must admit it. I am 'possessed' by my five cats. They have me wrapped around their little paws—and they know it! I work hard to provide them with shelter, food and water, and veterinary care. The necessities of life. I try to provide for the kitties as best I can while working a low paying job. It is not easy to get by sometimes.

They are not "just cats". They are my kids; so, you could say that I am their 'daddy'. I made the choice not to declaw them and each has been neutered. My house is a small one in a city and has five rooms. Each kitty has laid claim to their 'own' room. Each child deserves their own room, right?

All five kitties are strictly indoor only. I allow none of them to go outside . I would be very upset to find any one of my fur kids outside as roadkill or poisoned. It saddens me to see all the poor animals in the road that have been killed.

I am love my feline children. They have given me many years of companionship and love. I am hoping that I have many more years with them. A cat, (dog, or whatever pet one chooses), is a lifetime commitment. Through the good times and the bad.

My kids have provided me with both amusement and frustration. It can cheers me up when I am down to watch my children play with each other or their toys. They may even play with me. They just love to chase the laser "bug" all over the room.

It annoys me that they can't seem to learn to stay off the top of the table. (Especially when I am eating! Some foods are poisonous to our feline friends. While I make sure my cats have food, I don't wish to eat my food after they have had a bite of it. That doesn't mean that I love them any the less.)

Each of my children has their own distinct personality. They are all smart, too. I only had to show them where the litter boxes were only once. I have only had a few 'problems' in the five years that they have been here.

I don't like cleaning the litter boxes. I know that I am not alone. Many cat owners feel the same as I; like throwing up each time I do it. Yet, cleaning their litter boxes is an important daily chore. There will be less odors in the house, the kitty is less likely to mess in the house, and it is healthier for the kitty.

Let me describe my kids to you; presented in no particular order.

I'll start with Eeyore. He and his sister Tigger have owned me for about five years now. Eeyore is a short-hair, dark gray and slightly lighter gray striped tiger with some white on his belly, muzzle, and between his green eyes. I used to say to others that Eeyore looked so ugly that he is beautiful.

He is a quiet cat most of the time. Eeyore spends most of his time is napping. He will run and hide when a stranger comes into the house.

Yet, he is quite affectionate with me. Eeyore will not let many other people even pet him—much less touch him! He does occasionally play with Morkie or Pooh_B. He and Tigger used to be close when they were kittens; but, I don't see much interaction between them nowadays.

Eeyore knows how to get my attention. Should I be on the computer, (typing a letter, working on a spreadsheet, or surfing the Internet), he'll soon be sitting on my computer desk waiting for me to finish. If I don't get done soon enough for him, he'll start to ask for attention. He does this by coming over and laying a paw upon my forearm while meowing. I see him watching me with those wide eyes of his and my heart just melts. I lift him into my arms, petting him and he starts to softly purr.

His sister, Tigger, (also five years old), has emerald green eyes. She is mostly black with some very dark brown stripes on her sides with a spot or two of white on her belly and a white muzzle. I think she has one of the cutest feline faces I've ever seen.

Her fur feels different from Eeyore's, too. Whereas Eeyore's fur feels like cotton, Tigger's feels like soft silk or satin. Now that I think about it; each of the kitties' fur feels different from the others.

Tigger keeps mostly to herself. She really doesn't play that much with the other cats. She is my 'watcher' kitty. She likes to see what is happening in the house.

I can be doing something around home and suddenly feel like someone is watching me. I look around and there is Tigger staring at me. She also likes to observe what the other kitties (and the occasional stranger) are doing.

Tigger is not afraid to let you know when she wants something; usually it is food. She has a loud voice. Luckily, (especially at night), she'll only meow for a few minutes.

Pooh_B, also known as Pooh, is a solid yellow-orange long-hair about four years old. He has beautiful light green eyes and a very fluffy tail. His fur feels like cotton.

Pooh has an attitude, or catitude as some would say. He acts like he owns the place. Pooh will run through the house without an apparent care as to where he is going; sometimes actually colliding with things. He sleeps wherever he wants; usually someplace up high like the top of the dresser or cabinets. I have read that all cats like high places.

One may pet Pooh when he wants. He will come to you and say a single meow. If he doesn't start getting attention within a few minutes, he will walk off; tail held high.

When I try to pet Pooh when he doesn't wish it, he'll lower his head, lay his ears back, and look at you with an expression of 'leave me alone' on his face. Should you keep petting him, he'll eventually swat at you with his claws out. And, believe me, his claws are sharp!

My fourth master, Morkie, is a dark charcoal gray short-hair with yellow eyes. She looks like a Russian Blue. There are two small patches of white on her chest between her legs.

Morkie is the mischievous one. She acts like a kitten, always getting into things, even though she is one year old. She loves to play with empty bags and boxes, milk rings on the floor, catnip mousies, and catching insects. Mork runs through the house much more Pooh_B, chasing I don't know what.

Morkie will purr loudly when being petted. Her fur feels satiny soft. Morkie will also set on my shoulder, like a pirate's parrot while being petted. Mork takes after Tigger in that she isn't afraid to meow when she wants something. Sometimes, I think she meows just to meow.

My final owner is the most reclusive of all. She will only come out of her hiding place to eat or to use the litter box. She will growl and hiss at the other four cats if they are anywhere near her. It seems she doesn't want anything to do with them. Nor, is it often that I get to pet Sheba because she is such a recluse.

Sheba is 14 years old. She spends most of her time napping. She is a short-hair tortie with green eyes.

I now wish that I had had kitties around the house earlier in my life. I'll be 50 years old come November 2006. I never knew how much fun it could be having a cat could be until Eeyore and Tigger arrived.

I would recommend having a cat around the home to anyone who will take the time to love and be loved by the kitty. They deserve no less; and they will love you totally.

Cavebear's Muse
Cavebear

Cavebear is sitting at the computer, reading emails and posts, as usual. Suddenly a familiar "ding" comes from the ceiling lamp. It's not just a bulb burning out, it's my Muse making her personal presence known.

"Muse, would you please stop eating the bulb filaments when you show up? I mean, it's counter-productive. I have to replace too many bulbs, and besides, my eyesight is going. I know it's just a blink of a mortal eye to you, but I'm getting too old for this."

"Cavey dear," (oh man, I hate that wheedle in her voice, it means something new) "this time I want you to write about me." "You?" (I say stupidly; it is crystal-clear-cold like an icicle nailed through the foot.) "Yes," she purrs, "it is time for us to renew our contract; read the small print."

I read the small print, hurriedly: "Party of the first part," party of the second part," "Muse," "cavebear," "story-ideas," etc. Seemed normal, but then my eyes fell on a strange phrase. I asked Muse what "party of the 3rd "negative 'i' meant." Knowing my Muse, I wasn't going to like this one bit. Sure enough, it seemed that what I got from my Muse, she got from someone else, and that "someone else" wanted a raise in pay. This did not sound good!

"So," I said casually, "what does Mr. X want from me?" Muse just smiled, "Nothing you can't afford to pay," she stated thriftily; "Just a little extra that the Master really wants." Well, I wasn't born yesterday. I demanded specifics (and Muse whispered in my ear…)

Oh the ignominy of it all! I have to admit that the cost *is* truly small. Muses (and Muse Masters, it seems) don't really pay attention to currency anyway. They live on a different plane. It isn't money that drives them, it is those little creature comforts that we humans don't quite understand…

There is a creature that is not quite of this world that demands milk as payment for service. I think they were called "kobolds" or something like that. Anyway, in my case, I put down the small saucer of milk, as instructed by my Muse, and I backed away carefully. Instantly, LC, my cat, ran up to it and started to drink. As I started to shoo her away, she sat up and smiled at me.

Cats don't smile.

And I stopped the "shooing" motion immediately…

LC finished off the bowl of milk, and she returned to her spot on the table next to my computer. "How odd," I thought, "LC is always there when I am writing some story, yet my Muse leaves after I get the original idea." Hmmm…

I have the vague feeling that my contract with the Muse has been renewed… Through a "negative 'i' party," of course. I may start buying a better brand of catfood, too. And more milk.

Finding A New Home
Derby Sassycat

Friday, April 15, 2005

It was this day that I got taken to the Humane Animal Welfare Society (HAWS) in Waukesha, Wisconsin. It had all been so confusing lately. At times my owner had been forgetting things. Sometimes to take her pills, sometimes to feed me or clean my box. Her family was concerned and had been to visit lots.

Today was the mostest confusing day. Lots of people coming and putting things in boxes, but I wasn't allowed to play with them. Matter of fact, I got putted into special box and taken away from my home. As it turned out my firsted owner couldn't keep me any more as she was being moved into a nursing home. I wasn't allowed to go along and be a kittie nurse for her.

When I gotted to the shelter the people were furry nice, but I was real quiet. They checked me out from my nose to the tip of my tail, ears to the bottom of my paws. They even did tests on me for a while. Good news, no fleas, ear mites, and negative for feline leukemia and FIV. Then I was put into a cage all by myself. I was used to roaming a nice large place and now I only had a few feet to move in. I had a nice towel bed, food, water, a few toys and my litter box. Since I hadn't been getting much food lately, ate up all of the crunchies fast.

Over the next few days I settled into my new situation and then got moved into a new room that had lots of cages with lots of kitties in them. We were all in the same situation, hoping for a new home. So we shared our stories of our past lives. Kitties brought in from the farm, others whose owners who now had other people living with them who got the sneezies from having a kittie around. But we were all nice, just a bit down on our luck at the moment.

Over the next week or so, some kitties left as they founded new homes, others joined our group. All we could do was wait. Wait, and hope that one of the many people who would come in to look, would actually pick kittie to take home to love.

April 25, 2005

Today was the firsted day that I first spied the purrson who is now my mum. She came to the shelter and actually came in and looked at the kitties. She went from cage to cage, looking at our little information tags. These tags said how old each kittie was, gender, other interesting facts about us. Mum said she didn't want to adopt a kittie who was a barn or farm stray, as she didn't know how well they would adapt to being an inside only kittie. My little sign said I was a boy, (my name at the time was 'Benny', not exactly a thrilling name), one and a half years old, all four paws de-clawed. Being re-homed as my firsted owner was put into a nursing home.

But as she came through she would try to get each of us to play with her. Some of the kitties didn't move, but not me. When she moved the little mousie by the door, I jumped on it and stuck my paw out to say 'Hi'. But she moved on visiting with all of the kitties, but then she lefted.

I thought, what a nice purrson. Come back and play with me some more.

Friday, May 6, 2005

I was just relaxing after lunchtime and then this blonde lady came into the kittie room at the shelter. Hey, I remember her. She was here last week and played with me. She came over to say hello and I wanted to play with her. But then she also went down to play with another kittie named Mikey.

After a few minutes she left and I was disappointed we didn't get to play longer. Then a few more minutes and then one of the shelter people came in and took Mikey out of his cage. What I didn't know then was that the tech was taking Mikey into a special room to meet with this blonde lady.

About 15 minutes later they brought Mikey back, but then I gotted taken out of my cage. They took me to the special room and there she was, the blonde lady. Well, I figured now was the time for me to shine.

Firsted, I meowed 'Hello' and rubbed up against her. Then she had some toys and we had such a good time playing. We played for about 15 minutes and I thought this was so much fun. This blonde lady needs to come and play with us kitties every day.

But then this she lefted the room for a bit, and I was there by myself. I was ready to keep playing all afternoon. But then she came back and gave me some scritches and then said something very wonderful. "I'll be back for you tomorrow".

Ohh, Ohh, she would be back to play tomorrow. More play time.... or did she mean something else??

Saturday, May 7, 2005

I was so excited knowing that my blonde lady would be back. Our morning was pretty routine at the shelter with feeding and getting our cages cleaned.

But then after lunch all of a sudden one of the shelter techs came, took me out of my cage and into a back room. They gave me a stabby shot in the back of my neck. The tech was very nice and said she was giving me a chip to make sure I could be found, if I ever gotted losted. Then she put me inside a carrier, which had soft towels on the bottom and carried me out to the lobby.

The lobby had lots of people and was very noisy, but they sat me down on the floor and I looked up and there was my blonde lady. She leaned over and said hello. Then after a few more minutes, she gathered her stuff, some papers and **ME**!!!!!! She was taking me with her!!!!! She wasn't just coming to play with me she was taking someplace else to play.

She carried me out to her car and carefully loaded the carrier into the car and secured it with the seat belt.

Then got in and started the car. Plus she leaned over and said the the majic words to me. "Derby, lets go home". **HOME**, I was going to my new furever home. Plus I learned my new name, and I liked Derby better.

On the drive home, I did lots of talking. The blonde lady just kept softly talking to me. Saying we are going home, I love you, don't be scared. So after a bit I quieted down and even took a very quick nap.

Then the car stopped, the blonde lady got out and took some stuff in the house and then came and got me in the carrier. She just left me in the carrier for a few minutes while I adjusted to being inside. She got some food and water ready for me and then opened the carrier door right by the feeding bowls.

Well, I didn't waste any time. I came right out of the carrier, sniffed at the food and then went and jumped into the kitchen window. FREEDOM to wander!!! Very important to us kitties.

The blonde lady just watched me and let me wander around. So after checking out the kitchen, I did the family room, living room and then down to the dungeon. Down in the dungeon, I found my litter box. I just continued to check out the house for the rest of the day.

The blonde lady just left me do my thing, she worked on her house works stuff and laundry. Plus we watched the Kentucky Derby on TV. She didn't try to smother me or pick me up. But she did give me a few treats from her hand and scritches when I came around to sit by her. I felt so comfortable that by night I even jumped on her bed to sleep. Purrrrrrssss. It was a good night and I slepted real well and kept watch as well. I figured I had a keeper here and didn't want her to disappear.

The next morning, Sunday, I had been awake and 'sploring the house some more before anyone else was outta bed. I came up from the dungeon with my face full of spidey webs. Mum, yes I could call her mum now, laughed and helped get the mess off. She knew I had been in spots she didn't or couldn't get at to clean.

We just spent a quiet morning, me checking out the rooms mum hadn't closed the doors to, mum reading her newspaper. Then in the afternoon, I got to meet mum's Dad, Grampie. He was very nice, even though he kept calling me 'Gary'. He learned my correct name real soon.

Again, I felt safe and comfortable, with this nice blonde lady. Thanks for giving me a nice home, Mum. Purrrrs.

I'm gorgeous, I know you concur.
If the queen had a cat, I'd be her.
I am pampered I know,
And deservedly so.
Do not touch me; you'll mess up my fur
~Karl Schulz

How to Be a Blogging Cat
Sanjee

The bloggin world is not just for human beans any more! Thanks to bloggin cat pioneers like Psychokitty and Timothy Dickens, we cats have learned that we can blog too. A'course that is a real huge impurrovement over just plain old human bean blogging cuz we cats are superior creatures wif lots of opinions and lots of things to say.

So how do you become a bloggin cat? Easy! Just follow these easy steps to have your human bean cat staff to take care of the annoyin details. After all, that's what they's for, right? Yep, right!

1. Instrukt your cat staff to go to Blogger.com or another blog purrvider, and have them sign you up for a blog. If you haf brofur and sisfur cats, and you don't wanna take up too much time from your nappin and playin, try hafin a blog for all of youse at one time. Some cats purrfer this.

Make sure your staff uses your name instead of their own. It's not as if the blog will be about the cat staff anyways. Cat staff sumtimes forgets that it's not about them. (If your cat staff balks at such a simple task, perhaps you need to spend more time training your staff to obey your efurry command first.)

2. Instrukt your cat staff on how you want your blog set up.

You pick the template and colors you like, and things like that, and tell your staff to use them. Should your staff not understand what you's tellin them, you may need to hop up on the desk and actually put your paw on the pikshur of the template and colors you likes best. Sometimes cat staff isn't too sharp. If your help isn't furry computer literate, you may needs to enlist the help of a second cat staff to get this done pawperly. Use as many cat staff as needed to accomplish getting your blog set up.

3. Proof your cat staff's work while purraising them for their efforts, no matter how gross the errors are. We knows that cat staff just aren't as smart as us cats, but they tries hard. They requires lotsa purraisin to keep them from sulkin.

4. Instrukt your cat staff on how to fix their errors. We knows there will be sum, cuz of the staff just not bein cats. They can't help it, so try to be nice (relatively speakin) when instruktin them how to fix their screw ups.

At this point, if your cat staff has been obedient, you should haf a bloggy all ready fur you to tell the world what's on your superior kitty mind. So blog away, and share your feline wondermousness wif the world!

Some days finking is just too much trubble but you wanna blog anyways. After all, you can't disserpoint your fans. Here's some idears for your bloggin for days like that.

1. Stinky Goodness and crunchies. Always a yummy topic! Whefur you eats Fancy Feast, or Cat Chow, or somefin else, all cats likes to hear about stinky goodness.

2. Cat staff issues and tips. Let your bloggin cat furriends know they's not alone wif their cat staff problems. Help them out wif tips on how you handle your staff, too.

3. Pest control. From fleas to d-o-g-s to sticky little people, there's always some pests tryin to make our lives as purrfect cats diffycult. You can share how you copes wif such annoyin fings or just vent bout them annoyin you.

4. Feline facts. Us cats are interestin! Show 'em the facts about how interestin we are on your bloggy.

5. Treatsies. Treatsies are always furry poppylar. Temp-tay-shuns are the most popular wif bloggin cats, but bloggin cats luvs all kindsa treats.

6. Kitty romance. Romance is always a poppylar topic. Whefur you gots an online boyfriendcat, or are

hafin a sekrit affair wif the Persian down the street, enquirin cats wanna know.

7. Cat work. A kitty's work is nefur done! We hafta instrukt our staffs, keep the local d-o-g-s in line, groom, take eleventy naps a day, and all kindsa stuff. Tell your cat furriends what kindsa work you do that's so hard you need those eleventy naps a day.

8. Hunting. Caught any tasty birdies lately? Saved your staff from a vishus deer or a slinkin snakey? Howl your huntin' pride out!

9. Nipping it up. Partyin wif catnip makes for fun tails... um... tales.

10.   Kittens. Mom cats espeshully like hearin about kittens. They go "awww" a lot when you blogs about them.

Suggestions for Easy and Excellent Cat Bloggin

Dictate your blog posts to your cat staff. Typin can be hard on the paw pads since the silly keyboard manufakshurers make the keys so small. Use your cat staff's small paws and opposable thumbies for all they're worth.

Let the ofur kitties of the world see how wondermous you are wif pikshurs or movies. Instrukt your cat staff on how to take pikshurs or movies of you for your blog. They won't naturally know how to do this pawperly. You gots to show them which is your best side and what poses make you look slimmest. And unner no circumstances should you let your staff chase you around the house wif the flashy box, just cuz they want to. You's in control. You decide when to have photo shoots.

Be snarky but not too snarky. Psychokitty, one of those pioneer cat bloggers I mentioned earlier has snarkiness down to purrfection. Some snarkiness is good; it shows the world you's not a sissy panty-waist type of cat. Too much snarkiness can cause email erupshuns which are annoyin.

Occasionally, allow your cat staff to post on your blog. Just occasionally, mind you! The blog is about you, not your staff. Lettin them post on your bloggy once in a while makes them feel impawtant, tho, and this helps get the best work out of 'em. (Sneaky, huh?) It also shows what a benevvylent staff boss you are, efun if you's not really. (Also sneaky!)

Find ofur bloggin cats around the world to share stories and stuff wif. They's all ofur the place. Read ofur cat blogs to learn new tricks (NOT like sittin or beggin) on how to haf a fun bloggy experience. Goin to the *Carnival of the Cats* (http://www.carnivalofthecats.com) or *Weekend Cat Blogging* also are good ways to meet ofur kitties.

Have your cat staff put linkies to your favoritest cat blogs on your blog template. If you must haf links to human bean blogs or ofur critters, put them in a separate sekshun so that your furriends don't get confused about who your blog is really about.

Particypate in bloggin cat parties and contests and stuff. You can win the recognishun you so richly deserve, and sumtimes you can efun win catnip or ofur purrizes!

Ignore idiots unless you just wantsta fight. There's more idiots in the world than there are kitties, I finks. Sooner or later, an idiot's gonna comment on your bloggy. If you wantsta fight, sharpen your claws and go for it. Ofurwise, just ignore 'em. It annoys the dickens out of them. hehehe

Now you knows all about how to be a blogging cat. Go for it. We bloggin kitties are gonna rule the world a'fore you knows it!

~Sanjee, Queen of the House of the Mostly Black Cats, as dictated to Mom Robyn, Cat Staff

HAM.
Salty, sweet, wonderful HAM
That Pink Meat from heaven.
I don't know why I love it so much.
Shrimps are devine
Tuna is sublime.
Roast Beast is always wonderful.
Turkey is gobble-ishus
Chick-hen so tasty.
But HAM.
Oh HAM.
Oinky goodness.
~Miles Meezer

Kitty
Jane Schumacher

In the bag I sat on the floor.
Others walked in from the front door,
But they could not see me at all
Hidden from them in the long hall.

As I watched them, they look some more.
In the bag I sat on the floor.
They missed me hidden in plain view,
Watching them, if they only knew

Not suspecting, eyes on their backs
Raising the hair upon their necks.
In the bag I sat on the floor,
Holding position never sore

I'm a kitty waiting to play
With my people-what will they say?
"Love the kitty more and more."
In the bag I sit on the floor.

In Search of...
LC

The pond is ahead. I must wait carefully. I've been 'breadloaf', paws tucked under my front, disguising all threats. Waiting quietly, patiently, for 30 minutes, waiting for them to resume their activities. I'll hear them when they do. The least scratch or squeek alerts me. I sit so quietly, none can sense my presence at all. Even The Big Thing on the deck doesn't know where I am and he is looking right at me.

I am the leaf; the blade of grass; The mantis sitting on me knows not whereof it waits. I am the invisible part of the natural world. The kitty-zen of the universe surrounds me. I am the Tao and the Te; the Pi and the Phi. Delta and Omega. I am all and nothing. The universe surrounds me and I surround the universe.

I wait. Unmoving, silent, still as death, for death I am. I see the tiniest insects moving beneath me, around me, on me; it does not matter. I am hunting. I cease to exist. I could eat those little insects and they would not even know I existed, was aware. But I sit quietly. None must know of my slightest karma, my least breathe or my sensory emanations. I stop breathing…

I hear the least of sounds. My ears involuntarily radar forward. I gently and oh so carefully twitch them bring them into alignment. I suddenly find the source of that softest noise. It has entered my dry world!

Oh, be still my beating heart; my noisy lungs. Stop moving, my restless excitable tail. Become one with the universe. Accept the patience needed to not 'be here'! Black and White fur becomes the same as brown and red tree-fur fallen in the near cold time. "I am not here", "I am not here", "I am not here"!

Self fades from existence, the body flows into shadow, the mind stops until needed. I am not here…

Success! I vanish… I must not celebrate, lest I return. Quiet, quiet, all is stillness. I wait, part of and not part of the material world, not even thought of, imagined to be gone. So quiet and patient. Waiting…

Good, I am still out of the world. None can see me, smell me, detect my existence. I wait longer…I hear more slight creeping curious sounds. My prey is resuming it's business. It is quiet oh so quiet and careful. I hear it, but it does not sense me. "I am not here"", "I am not here", "I am not here"!

And I am not. It scales the sides of the pond slowly, watchfully. The least shadow or sensation of existence would cause it to leap away. It is even more cautious than I am. Dinner for me, life for it…. A challenge of us two to see which is least "here".

It looks for the shadow of heron, the shape of snake, the least new position of anything. But I am not here…It sees nothing, cannot see anything, for I am not to be seen. I am the tree-stump here for months, the fallen branch unmoving for weeks. I am that which is not present. It creeps slower than grass grows , looking for a moth or beetle to snatch and flee with. I wait…

It reaches the top of the pond. I tense, thinking of every tiny muscle, knowing every body movement to be, every ligament and tendon, every claw, willing them all to work in sudden unison when I am prepared to act. When I have utter complete control of every part of me to the last fur, I return to the world and I spring.

I HAVE THE FROG! It complains mournfully in my mouth as it releases it's pee into the universe hoping to get me to release it. But I know how to grab these things. I swish it in the pond and carry it to the open lawn…

So it's salmon tonight? What a bore:
You've served it this week twice before,
So I'll sniff it and then
Turn my nose up again
As I regally stalk to the door.

~Karl Schulz

Noir Chat
Merlin

I sat in the shadows of the damp wall watching the street rats scramble through paradise's garbage and waited. The smoke from my cigarette curled lazily through the air, wrapping around the palm fronds like VOG blown in by the Kona winds from the big island. She hadn't shown herself yet, but I had all night. I could stand here smoking like a broken chimney until the sun broke over the mountains if I had too. It made no difference to me, in the dark on the street or in the dark of my kitty cubby, that's what I had to look forward too.

Music drifted over from the open bar competing with the sound of glasses on wood and voices mouthing words that ran together like waves over sand, distilling into individuality only often enough to keep the conversation flowing fast as the niptinis.

I saw her walk into the bar and perch on stool over by the flaming tiki torches. She caught the bartender's reptilian eye quick enough. She had that effect on a person. It could be the bewitching green eyes or maybe the shy smile shaded by stunning white whiskers polished to a sheen, or maybe not. All I know is when she entered a room, everyone noticed, and when she entered a room containing just one other, she overwhelmed.

Three days ago, was it that soon? It felt like forever since she had darkened the door of my cathouse, leaning casually against the rope covered post and brushing the dangling stuffed mouse out of her face. She smiled when she saw me sitting there gapping like a fish out of water or a cat caught unawares, which I was.

"I need your help," she purred in low contralto that caused sweet vibrations of the hair along my spine.

"Uh, sure," I replied rather stupidly, but what else was there to say? Sorry I don't help strange cats, especially ones decked out in diamond collars. I'm not that stupid.

She smiled that shy smile and vamped her way across the cube, shedding white fur as she moved. "Oh good. I heard you were dependable."

From whom, I wondered as she sat close enough to brush whiskers with me. Obviously this dame hadn't heard of personal space, but I wasn't going to complain. "So tell me about it doll. What can I do for you? Find a missing collar, uncover a stolen earring, track down an errant tail ring?"

"No silly. I have all my jewelry." I noticed a slight lisp to her speech. "I need you to get back a letter that was taken from me."

"Why don't you just ask for it back?" I quizzed her, thinking that maybe looks and intelligence really didn't go together that often. After all, not everyone could be a blessed as me. I chuckled.

"Don't laugh," she pouted. "It's serious. There's information in the letter of a personal nature that I don't want others seeing."

I coughed as she laid her head on my chest fur and looked up into my eyes, hers expanding into large round circles as big as the moon shining in the window and over my cat cube. "Will you get it for me?" she asked.

"Sure, sure, I'll get back your love letter for you. Just let me know who took it."

~

Yep, that was three days ago and since then I had been chased by wild pigs, snapped at by rampant dogs, thrown over board, and almost run over. This is not how my life was supposed to go.

I fondly reminisced about sleeping in the windows in the sun and snoozing in my cat basket, climbing my cat tree, and enjoying stinky goodness in my special bowl. Oh those were the days. Now I didn't know what was going to happen from one minute to the next, but I knew I was going to find out, and the answer lay with Miss fur-coat-sparkly-collard-sultry-voice-Slinky-eyes. Yes I forgot to ask her name, but I new a set up when I was in one.

So there I was standing in a smelly alley watching and waiting, while cockroaches scuttled passed on their way to the bug buffet.

This dame could talk let me tell you and the night was moving on. Just about the time I was ready to curl up and take a quick cat nap, a big Burmese cat with mean looking eyes stalked in and went up to her table. Before anyone could say a how-de-doo, Ms. Slinky excused herself and pranced out of the bar followed by the cold glance of the gecko bartender, slitty-eyes glowing with reflected light.

My pulse quickened with the hunt as I followed the pair down the street, wearing the shadows like second skin. They didn't go far, stopping at the docks. The murky water lapped in odorous rhythm as the three of us stood expectantly waiting. I wondered why as I leaned against a rough wall.

I didn't have long to wait before a canoe, rowed by two mangy poi dogs, slid quietly up to the dock. Sitting in the back like a hairy Buddha was the fattest wild pig I have ever seen. He was huge. His little piggy eye glowed yellow as if lit from within. And I thought the Burmese looked mean!

There was no chitchat. The dogs hopped out and unloaded a crate at the feet of Ms. Slinky and her henchcat.

"Okay," gunted Pig, "Where's the papers? I need proof of delivery for my boss. Plus I need to know you are who you says you are."

Ms. Slinky gave a nervous laugh. "Um, I seem to have misplace them. I can be so careless sometimes. Leave the box and I promise I will get the papers to you soon."

"You have 24 hours Miss." squeaked Pig, the underlying menace of the oily voice hung in the muggy air. Without a word the dogs settled back into the canoe and rowed off.

As the big Burmese hunched over to check inside the crate, Ms Slinky gave a nervous glance around. "Come on, not here. I have a.........." She didn't have a chance to finish her sentence as I strolled out from the shadows, trying for a blasé look but achieving no more than eavesdropper status.

"What are you doing here?" she gasped.

The Burmese proved to be a cat of even fewer words as he turned and jumped on me with a spine tingling howl. The fight was on. He was good. I cringed as I felt his claws scratch and catch my skin. Tufts of fur flew. Howls filled the night air. We rolled. We spat. We bit and clawed.

After what seemed like an eternity to my battered body, but was probably only minutes, the Honolulu Police Department drove up, sirens matching our screeches on the air. The Burmese jumped off and took off into the breaking dawn. Ms. Slinky just stood and stared for once speechless.

"Alright miss, put your paws up and step away from the crate." Ms Slinky glared at me reproachfully as she complied.

"I can't believe you turned me in," she pouted.

"All in a days work sweetheart," I shot back. "Try and take me for a fool."

While HPD officers read Ms Slinky her rights, cuffed her, and put her in the back of the police car, I slowly opened the crate lid.

Scrunched up in a corner, shaking with fear were four bundles of fluff. Eight eyes squinted at me in the morning light as fear shone out.

"It's gonna be okay little guys. You can go home now." I felt like I was offering a sip of water to dehydrated explorer, not enough, but at least something.

Later that week, I found myself sitting in the Black Cat dinning room, waiting for my friend from HPD. He shuffled in late apologizing as he sat down. "Not to worry," I said sipping my niptini and munching on cat treats.

"I'm supposed to offer you off the record concatulations for breaking up that kitten smuggling ring. The chief can't make it official, but he sends his thanks." My friend ordered a salmon catgrass salad and nip beer.

Tuna Juice

Did I hear the can?
Do you smell the feast?
I see you are making Tuna today
Don't forget to share the juice

-Mia

Forever Home
Mia

It was a very confusing time. I had been living with the two boys. I had never been outside. One day they started moving things around and putting things in big boxes. Then they let me and Brownie go outside. I didn't know what to make of it. It was exciting first. Then it got a lil' scary. I waited for the boys to come back but they didn't. I saw a nice lady in the yard next door and I ran to her and asked her if she had anything to eat. I was hungry. She looked at me a long time and told me that she didn't have anything to give me. I was sad. Later she came back and she had some crunchy stuff. Me and Brownie would eat and drink on her porch. She kept putting the crunchy stuff out and we kept coming back.

A few days later, the boys came back and I was excited. I saw the lady talking to one of them. I thought I heard her ask if they were going to take me and Brownie with them. I don't know what he said to her but he didn't take me or Brownie anywhere. A little later the other boy came back and picked up Brownie and then it was just me.

The lady seemed to be unhappy about something but she kept giving me the crunchy stuff. I wondered when the boys were coming back.

One evening, a few days later, I was laying out on the cool cement and the lady came and picked me up and brought me into her house. I hadn't been in house before and it was just as well. There was a giant dog in the house. As big as a horse. I was so scared. I had never met a dog before. The lady hugged me tight and took me into one of the rooms and closed the door. I was very scared. As soon as she put me down, I hid under the bed. I stayed there the whole night. In the morning, the lady gave me some crunchy stuff and then carried me to the car. This was the first time I have ever been in a car. It was horrible. The whole car smelled like the giant dog in the house.

The car ride was bad, but where we ended up was definitely worse. The V-E-T. The beans were very sweet and friendly, but they poked and prodded me and stabbed me. Ouchie! When the lady came back to get me, I was super happy to see her, she took me home. On the way, she told me that she was going to take care of me and make sure that nothing bad happened to me.

"What about the giant dog?" I said.

"The dog won't hurt you", she said.

I was skeptical. The dog was 9 feet tall and weighed 124 lbs. Well, maybe not 9 feet, but he really did weigh 124 lbs, and compared to my 8 lbs, I was toast.

When we got back to the house, the lady put me in my own room with my own dishes for crunchy goodness and water and my own private litter box. She put a gate in the doorway to keep the horsedog out. I eyed him from behind the gate as he was trying to inhale me with his giant nostrils.

The next morning, the lady bean and the guy bean left the house. The left me in the room behind the gate with the door closed. The horsedog was sniffing at the bottom of the door. I tried to swipe at him with my paw, but I couldn't get it under the door because the gate was there. He sniffs a little longer and then stops. I jump on this skinny table that is really close to door. It's a little wobbly but I sit at the edge.

I

can

almost

reach

the

door.

I stretch my right paw out and I touch the door. You're not going to believe this; the door swings outward, away from the gate and opens. I'm sitting on the wobbly table and all I have to do to get out of the room is jump off the table and over the gate.

I'm out! I'm walking around checking out the house. Ol' Horsedog comes lumbering over and I freeze. He sticks his big nose in my face, but I'm scared and run away; he tries to run after me, but I find out that I'm so much faster than him. I realize then that I don't have to be afraid of him because I'm always going to be able to get away from him. I can hide in places he can't reach. I continue my explorations of the house. There's lots to smell and lots to see. I find a window in the front and watch the squirrels in the yard. I decide to take a nap.

The next thing I know, the guy bean comes home.

He sees me out of my room and he says to me, "Well, I guess you're out now, there's no use putting you back behind the gate."

That's what I'm talking about! I had free reign of the house from that day on. I got to know the dog better. His name was Ragamuffin, but he said I could call him Rags. He was really relaxed. I liked to play with his tail. His tail was an animal in itself. It had to have been at least half his length. And it was super long; thick and furry. It wasn't bushy like a squirrel, but shaggy. I would pounce on it when he was sleeping and he wouldn't even wake up. The worst thing that he ever did to me was try to sniff my bum. That was very rude! I told him so and he apologized.

He said, "That's what dogs do."

I only knew my woofy, Ragamuffin, for one year, but he was good to me and never hurt me. Did I mention how ginormous he was? He went to the bridge on September 4, 2005. My beans and I were heartbroken. He got sick with bloat and went to the bridge unexpectedly.

He liked to sit in the front room with me when I watched the birdies and the buggies and the squirrels. He liked the squirrels. He almost caught one once, but Mr. Squirrel was lucky to escape at the very last moment. Soon we got to know each other better and would sniff each other politely. I liked sniffing his paws and pouncing on his tail, which was so long, it was like a snakey. He would sniff me nose to nose and sometimes chase me in the house to play but I always got away. He would let me chase my loop toy all over the house like a cat possessed and not try and take it from me. He liked my 'nip toys and would try to eat them, but beanmom always saved them.

He was a good woofy. I got to go outside with him and eat grass. He protected us from the crazy man who comes to the house most days and stands at the window, leaves some envelopes and then goes away. I hope that I will be OK without him. He was a good woofy to me.

Soon after Rags went to the bridge, a hurricane came to Houston, which is where I live. I didn't know what a hurricane was at the time, and I wasn't too concerned. My beans were very concerned. They packed up the house and took me to my bean grammie's house. At my grammie's house, I watched the news on the TV while we waited for the storm. I really wasn't too concerned about the storm because I was too busy inspecting grammie's house. She had an upstairs and a downstairs and I liked running up and down the stairs. There were so many interesting places for me to investigate. I found a secret napping spot at grammie's house that was the absolute bestest. I would go there to nap and mom could not find me and then I would appear again. She said that I vanished into thin air. We waited for the storm to come. Beanmom was a little scared but I was not.

I just did my nails to pass the time. The lights flicked on and off a little on Friday night, but I wasn't scared because I have super poodie vision. When the wind finally started I went to the window to watch but beanmom told me not to and took me away from the window. I went to my secret spot to watch the wind and then it started raining but not much. Mom was all a nervous because she's never been through a hurricane before. Me neither! But it wasn't so scary. On Saturday, beandad went back to our house to check on it and said that everything was fine, so we packed up all the stuff again and beanmom took me in the car again and brought me home. I enjoyed my visit to grammie's. And I hope I get to go and visit again soon. I think the worst part of the whole experience was the car ride to and from grammie's house.

Two days after the hurricane came, my other grambeans came to stay with us. The were the bean parents of my beanmom. They had come to visit because beanmom and beandad were going to get married the next week! There were so many strange beans coming in and out of our house. I didn't like it one bit. I snuck out of the house just to get a break from all the commotion. Beanmom didn't like that one bit. I was only at the house next door, so I don't know why she was so upset with me. She could see where I was. I just wasn't used to all the people and the commotion. She got me back into the house after a while. After a few days, there were fewer beans that were visiting and then my grambeans left as well. It was back to being just Beandad, Beanmom and me.

After Rags went to the bridge, I was alone with my beans. I was lonely at first, but I got used to being by myself. I could lounge luxuriously wherever I pleased during the day when my beans were at work. I had a lovely year to myself until Tigey showed up. Tigey is a cat. A big boy cat with a Belly Flap. My beans rescued Tigey, who had been living with beandad's auntie, when her house burned down. Auntie and Tigey were not hurt in the fire but the house didn't make it.

It took me a little while to get used to having Tigey,

another cat of all things, in the house. When he first came to live with us, he was a little sicky and mom had to take good care of him. He is doing just fine now and he can be a bit of a bully, but then, so can I. He likes to pounce on me and wrestle. I like to pounce on him and wrestle too. He's OK. I licked his head the other day and he pounced on me. That's not going to stop me from licking his head again!

Hah!

I'll lick your head as and when I please.

I'm happy that I picked my beans to take care of me. I knew they were the beans for me when I first saw them. I love my beandad and my beanmom and maybe Tigey. Well, OK, I do love Tigey, but lets just keep that between you and me. After all, I have a reputation to protect.

Derby Sassycat
admire you in secret
no more will I do

~Mia

Mouse Goes Hunting
Karen Jo Gray

A kitty named Mouse used to live up the street from me. He was a very handsome gray and white Tuxie and a mighty hunter. I was walking home from town one afternoon and saw him on the green area across the street from where he lived in full stalking mode. I stopped to watch, mostly because I didn't want to disturb him. At first, I couldn't figure out what he was stalking, because I couldn't see anything else on the green, except a very large raven. It didn't take me long to see that Mouse was stalking the raven. The closer he got, the slower he went. I thought he was slowly realizing just how big this bird was. All of a sudden, the raven spotted Mouse. The raven leaped up into the air, spread his wings, then swooped on Mouse. Mouse didn't hesitate. He ran hell for leather for home with the raven in full pursuit. Mouse made it to his front porch and the raven landed on the porch roof. As I walked on, Mouse was meowing and scratching at the door and the raven was scolding him from the roof.

The Skeeter
<>(apologies to Edgar Allan Poe) <>
Mark Spencer

Once upon a mid-day dreary, while I sat a-chair and
weary
Watching many old and samely TV shows of nature
lore,
'Mongst the naps and heady noddings, suddenly there
came a yawning
As of someone daytime dawning, yawning there upon
the floor.
"Tis a kitty-cat" I mutterred, "sitting there upon the
floor –
Only that and nothing more. <>

Easily I now remember it was in the chill November,
As the sullen silent weather outside thrust upon the
door.
Quietly I wished the bedtime, - but awaited anime-
time
For to see the wondrous graphics of the Nippon
paradigm
-
For the Futurama Bender and the Ghost within the
Shell –
Watching them in pixel hell.

<>As the kitty watched below me, watching as my legs
crossed briefly
Thrilled him – filled him with a want to sit upon my
lappy well;

And so then, my happy waiting of a lap that needing filling
Come up Skeeter, called I smiling, fill my lap an hour or more-
Come up now and fill my lap, fill it for an hour or more –
Only that, and nothing more.

<>Thereupon, I felt a presence, Skeeter standing off the floor,
Paws on leg as if in begging, then a launch and tour de force
Skeeter standing on my lap and curling up there with purrs amore.
And so gently he ascended, hardly he disturbed my senses
Happily asconced in warmth of what it is he so adores
–
˗

Warmth of shelter, trusting, melter,
Master of the lap domain.

<>Sleepy now, my fav'rite Skeeter, trusting loving mothie eater
Curls upon his human heater, sure he there will long abode.
And as human Skeeter heater, loving catlike warmth anon,
I'll not move, my pretty kitty, not until the light of dawn.
Only then and not before…

I Wanna Be Friends
Buddah

I am a little kitty
As black as black can be
Pretty soon I'll turn two
And after that comes three

I have a brother kitty, Max
He's five and thinks he's king
He bosses me around a lot
I cannot do a thing

Down the stairs he pushes me
And my food he tries to steal
But I know what he doesn't know
I know his Real Deal

He thinks he's snarky to the core
And really, really mean
But Max is just a grumpy guy
Who doesn't want his good side seen

Deep down Max really loves me
And he loves the Mom and Dad
He loves the Younger Human, too
So he can't be all that bad

That's what I tell myself each day
As he growls and swipes at me
As I tumble down the stairs
I say Hey look at me

I'll play with you and let you win
I won't tell you you're a nut
I'll just wait until you're deep asleep
Then I'll bite you on the butt

Max just snorts and turns away
He'd laugh if he only could
I know he wants to play with me
I really wish he would

Someday Max will think it's fine
To be my friend; we'll see
By then I may be four years old
But I hope it's only three.

No Name
craziequeen

He doesn't have a name. He's only little and a shade on the scraggy side.

He went for a walk with his mummy and some-how got left behind in this wonderful place. It's seems to be a holding place for humans—lots of them, mostly wearing just skin and none of the usual coverings. There he was, having a good sniff around on his first morning and suddenly huge humans overshadowed him. They went away and more arrived, clicking their tongues and waggling their fingers at him. It was very scary.

He retreated under the bush where he'd stayed since his mummy had disappeared when suddenly a little grey and white face appeared through the leaves.

"Bonjour," said the little face. "My name is Petit Chat –what's yours?"

"What's a name?" He asked, confused.

"Everyone has a name," said the little face. "It's a way of identifying each other to make sure we know who's who. My mummy is called Couleur and my little sister is called Petite Couleur. I have two big uncles called Nez Noir and Nez Blanc—they live over there" (the little face swung a glance across the blue water and screaming humans.) "Don't you have a name?"

"I suppose not," he replied. "Have you seen my mummy today?"

"No," Petit Chat answered. "But I can show you to my mummy and she'll look after you. But" he added quietly. "Watch out for Petite because she's just come out of the den and she's very playful!!"

He led the stranger to another bush where his mummy and sister were sleeping.

They all seemed to sleep an awful lot, He guessed it was the strain of meeting all those intrusive humans day after day. He didn't know how they resisted the urge to shake the humans by the scruff. Nosy humans.

Petit Chat gently cuffed his mummy and she hissed as she opened her eyes.

"What now?" she asked wearily, looking over to check on Petite with a quick lick for sure. "Aren't you old enough to look after yourself, Petit Chat? I've told you all…"

Her voice tapered off as she caught sight of him. He didn't look so hot, what with his blue eyes and ropy grey and white fur sticking out in all directions, but his eyes held a ray of hope as he watched the elder cat take in his appearance.

"*What* is that?" The words came out as a growl, and her eyes became icy.

"He's my new friend," said Petit Chat. "I found him this morning. Can he stay?"

He gently kneaded his mummy to put his point across. She batted him away harshly.

"He's not one of us," she hissed and spat at the young kitten. "He doesn't belong here, this is our home. Any old kitten can't waltz in here and take up residence. You should know that, Petit Chat! The man in uniform only puts out enough food for us. You expect us to share? And what about the beach cats, Albert and Georges? You've seen your Uncles have some terrible fights to ensure our privacy. I will not have Petite Couleur usurped either, she's the baby—my baby. Now get rid of him or I'll break his neck."

With those angry words she turned her back and groomed her belly. Amid the noise Petite Couleur woke up. She yawned, rolled over, and saw the newcomer.

"Mummy, there's strange kitten here!" she yelped and promptly ran and hid under her mother.

"Get a life!" Petit Chat exclaimed impatiently. "Look, he's smaller even than Petite. His mummy left him behind and he's all alone. Can't we at least keep an eye on him?"

The scrappy little kitten held his breath, one paw slightly raised in anticipation. Would he get a new family, or would he be cast out –or worse?

Petite Couleur peered from behind her mother. Her little eyes took in the tiny scrap, pathetic and hungry. She licked a paw in readiness and then sneaked her kittenish belly over the dry grass and sand and gently spoke. "Do you want to play with me, NoName?"

Out of the Shadows
Donna Olsen

The young cat woke and stretched, her boy kitten draped across her, warm and purring. She'd had that nightmare again, except that, it wasn't a nightmare, it was her life. She remembered at a mere six weeks being taken away from her mother. She remembered the house, the noisy kids, always yelling, hitting, and throwing things. She remembered coming face to face with the giant of a dog. It was then that it happened; she was so frightened she had left a puddle right were she stood. The large, loud man had grabbed her and tossed her out of the house onto the back porch! For the first few weeks they had filled a dish with dry kibble for her in the morning. Then it became every couple of days, with all the other animals that ate from her dish it was never enough. She started hunting the small wood behind the house. Then it happened, she met The Tom, she was only four months old and already half starved, her litter of three didn't survive long after being born.

The summer went its way and the cold began to come, first only at night, then every day. She was never warm, never had a full tummy and was always wary of predators. She lost the tips of her ears to frostbite; her paws became hard and calloused. Prey got harder to come by and more and larger predators started taking the small rodents and rabbits on which she had been subsisting. She lived in fear and hunger through that winter, three cold brutal months.

She met The Tom again. This time she found a small shed full of mice and soft rags to make a bed. She set up housekeeping, being careful not to be seen coming and going for here there were the dreaded humans again. In time she gave birth to three kittens, two male tigers and a little girl who looked like her. A soft, muted calico color.

The people here, though, were quieter than her first humans were. The children, a boy and a girl, didn't yell or throw things. They played chase and laughed. Then they saw her, she just had to sneak a peak at the giggling children. She ran for the woods, she didn't want them to find her babies. She stood, just inside the trees, and watched as the little girl crouched and called softly "here kitty, are you hungry?" She didn't go to her, just stood and watched. Eventually the boy came back with a tall lady; they put a bowl on the side of the shed and filled it with food. Oh, it smelled wonderful and her stomach growled from the hunger. However, she couldn't take the chance that they might hurt her, or worse, her babies. She waited until dark, and ate until she thought she would burst. For the first time since she had been tossed out she was full. She went back to her kittens and nursed them, warm and comfortable.

This went on for a number of days into weeks,

always when she got up in the morning the food dish was full. In addition, if she, or some other critter, emptied it during the day, it would be filled again. Eventually she stopped running every time someone stepped out of the house. They never chased her, like the other kids had, and no one ever yelled. She started to let the children sit near her and watch her, sometimes she would play chase the hair ribbon with the girl. Then came the day she let herself be touched, oh it felt so good. The gentle caress along her back, the wonder of having her sore ears rubbed. She let them do it every day and it felt GOOD.

Her kittens were starting to explore and now she knew she could trust these people. She brought them into the back yard one day and stood proudly showing off her fine offspring. "Oh, goodness" the lady was astounded that she had kept these little ones a secret for weeks. Something had to be done; these cats needed veterinary care and medicine. One of the boys had an infection in his eyes; all three had kitty colds and fleas. So a plan was devised, the food kept getting moved, closer and closer to the house, until one day it was on the porch.

She hadn't noticed that the bowl was in a large wire box. She walked right in, and was trapped. She cried, her babies, they were still in the shed. She would lose them, she would be hauled off to who knows what fate and never see her children again. Then the door opened and all three kittens were place inside with her, the cage was lifted. She felt something moving around her and under her; she felt a lot of bumping and swaying. Then the cage was lifted again and…oh horrors, here there were dogs! This time she kept her composure, but the kittens didn't and no one said bad words or threw any of them out. She was taken out and given a shot, she fell asleep. When she woke up, her middle was sore and she was wearing a big thing around her head and HER BABIES WERE GONE. No, not gone, she heard them in the cage next to her. She saw that they were getting medicine put on them. The same man who had given her the shot was holding them and cleaning their ears and eyes. A lady came and gave her food and then the tall lady and the children came and took them all back to the house with the shed.

Oh the house, she had toys and a bed all her own. Good food every day and soft pets and ear and chin rubs. And she now had a name, Sadie. Eventually all three of her babies were taken away and brought back with the same silly collar she had worn. She was home. She had come out of the shadows and found a forever home for herself and Tom, Jerry and Princess. Oh, and Tom still likes to sleep draped across his mom, some things never change.

As I walk all alone through the night,
I'm occasionally challenged to fight,
But most often a yowl
From down deep in my bowel
Puts my erstwhile opponent to flight.
                                                    -Karl Schultz

Thoughts of a Pet Owner
Dee Francis

I would like to share my thoughts of what it means to be a pet owner. I feel that all pets, whether they be a cat, dog, horse, rabbit, parrot, etc, should have some basic rights in the family. There are two reasons that I say this.

One, my consideration of what has been written about animal intelligence and consciousness. Two, my own observations of my five kitties.

Do pets have a consciousness, an awareness of their environment like humans? Scientists aren't sure. Research has shown hints that animals may indeed be aware. I have personally noticed that cats, (and dogs), seem to know the difference between wet and dry, hot and cold, pleasure and pain, happiness and sadness.

I do not know if animals reason things out like us humans. Nor do scientists. We have all heard stories of the kitty who waited until the right moment to bolt through the open door to escape outside or about the doggy that somehow learnt how to unhook his collar. The same situation applies to their emotions; though, as

I said above, pets seem to know happy from sad. I would say that they do possess feelings.

But, I stray from the subject at hand: what I would consider the basic rights of pets. However, these ideas play a part in my deliberations upon how to treat a pet.

First, when a person gets a pet (cat, dog, horse, etc.), the person should realize this is a lifetime commitment. With proper care, a pet will provide you with many years of companionship and unconditional love. They are not toys—to be played with and put back on the shelf when you're done. Nor, are they disposable; to be thrown away when the newness wears off. Or, you tire of them.

Second, pets should live in a clean and safe environment. Pets are not in your home to be tortured or abused. Kitties need their litter boxes scooped (and occasionally changed) every day. Doggies need to time to go outside and relieve themselves. All pets need to be stimulated with play. And, so do you!

Pets should also have clean water and food everyday. You want to keep your kitty or doggy healthy. They are members of your family and should be treated as such.

Pets should also have access to medical care. Especially when they are ill. Be aware that your pet can not tell you with words what is wrong with them. The only hint that you may see that they are ill may be peeing, (or pooping), on the carpet. (When they usually go outside or use the litter box.) Throwing up their dinner is another sign. A sudden change in their behavior is another tip-off. Get your pet to the veterinarian right away! Regular visits to the vet also helps keep your doggy (or kitty) healthy.

Please, dear reader, follow these simple rules for dealing with your pet. As I have said earlier, you take care of your pet; he (or her) will take care of you with many years of unconditional love, companionship, and happy memories.

The Storey of My Life
Skeezix the Cat

My name is Skeezix the Cat
and this is the storey of my life (so far)

I am two yeers old. I'm a big boy now. I liv in Castro Valley by the big forest with Mr Tasty Face, the Food Lady, my big bruther Mao, Rocky the Gutter Cat, and Tripper the Stray Cat. I didn't always liv heer. Win I was a baby I livd with diffrint peeple and my byootiful sisters. That's ware the Food Lady came to git me to bring me to liv with her. She was going to take one of my byootiful sisters. But then she talked to the lady I was living with and sed she reely wood rather have a boy cat. The old lady sed she had a boy cat, but he had bad cullering and he was a runt, and his cote wasn't vary thik, altho he did have a lot of persunality. That boy cat wuz me. The minit the Food Lady saw me, she knew I was the wun. I climed on top of her sholder and purred so lowd I thot my purrer wood brake. Yoo see, I knew the chances that sumwun wood pik me weren't vary good, so win I got my chance, I reely had to werk it. The Food

Lady put me in a box and took me to liv with her and Mr Tasty Face.

Win I ferst met Mr Tasty Face, he wuz vary sad. His faverit cat, Joonyer (hoo was my big bruther Mao's reel bruther) had just gone away to the ranebow brij. It was rite before Krismiss, and it made evrywun vary sad to have to have Krismiss withowt Joonyer. So the Food Lady surprized Mr Tasty Face by giving me to him as a Krismiss prezint. At ferst, Mr Tasty Face wuz upset. He duzn't like surprizes vary much, and he wuzn't reddy for anuther cat. And he coodn't beeleeve how ugly I was. So I werked my majik on him and made him like me. (Agin, I had to werk it.) I climed on his sholder and purred and purred and purred. Then I likt his face until I neerly likt it off. (That's how he got the name Mr Tasty Face. In fakt, his face was so tasty, I started a habit of likking it evry singul day.) I knew that he was the one I needed to impress if I was going to stay at this new howse in Castro Valley by the big forest. And altho he was still sad, I made him a littul happy. Purring duz that. He let me stay and I've bin thare ever since.

Win I ferst met my big bruther Mao, he wuz vary sad. He and Joonyer were Simeeze twins, praktikly. They had the same mommy and daddy, but they were born in diffrint litters. They had a kunekshun. Win Joonyer wint away, my big bruther Mao got deprest. He didn't have anywun to sleep with, or groom, or say hey to in the morning. Win the Food Lady brot me home, Mao didn't hate me. He started grooming me rite away, just like my Mom used to. So I started nursing on him. It was an

onist mistake. Mao was not wild abowt the nursing thing
and he hist and then he hit me. So I don't nurs on him
anymore. My big bruther Mao is the bestest big bruther
in the werld. He teeches me things like how to be a pikky
eeter, and how to wake the peeple up in the morning so
we'll git brekfist before noon, and how to projekt my
voice frum the bottum of the stares and stuff like that.

I didn't meet Rocky the Gutter Cat for a long time
becuz he was an owtside cat and I was an inside cat. Rocky
and Joonyer were vary best frends. Win Joonyer wint
away, Rocky got deprest too, just like Mao. That's win
Rocky desided he wunted to liv alone owtside. The inside reminded him of Joonyer and that made him sad.
The peeple tride to make him stay inside the howse, but
he sed no way and he peed on evrything in site. So they
finely gave up. Rocky likes hanging owt in the gutter,
wich is his new home. In the summer, he offin stays at
his summer home in the driveway insted of the gutter
becuz thare is lots of water in the gutter frum lons gitting
watered with sprinklerz. Rocky duz a lot of nip, and he
likes to go down to Spanky's, wich is a divebar ware
bikers with tatts drink likker. I think he smokes, too,
altho I've never akshully seen it with my vary own eyes.
It's just that sumtimes he smells funney, and I put 2 and
2 together.

The ferst few days in my new home in Castro Valley by the big forest were nice. I didn't miss my byootiful
sisters too much becuz Mao was a good big bruther. I
got to sleep in the peeple bed on a speshul tiny pillow
becuz they thot I'd freeze to deth in the cat bedroom. It

was winter, after all. In the middle of the nite I wood burro all the way under the cuvvers in the peeple bed ware it was nice and warm. Uzhully, that was grate, ixsept for the nites win they ate Mexican food and beens, wich made it stinky thare under the cuvvers. Mr Tasty Face didn't sleep so good, becuz he was werried abowt rolling over and sqwarshing me. That's win I started to sleep in my own bed in the cat bedroom. It has a heeting pad bilt in to keep me toasty, with a sheepskin floor and a sheep-skin "seeling" and a furry thing inside I can cuddle with. It's like a big berrito bed. I'm a burrower, so I like it!

Then I got sik. I had a respertorey infekshun. That's win I made my ferst trip to Bullevard Pet Hospital. This ment I got to ride in the blue plastik prizzin box, wich I didn't like so much. In fakt, I kind of hated it. I got torcherd with needles and they gave me barfy medisin, and goo to put in my eyes. It was the low point of my life.

And then, just a cuppul of days later, I got whut they call "konstipatid." That ment that the poop stade inside of me instead of going owt my poophole like it's supost to. It got uncomfterbul and I started to git hot. So it was bak in the prizzin box for me, but this time we had to go to the emerjinsy vet instead of Bullevard Pet Hospital, becuz it was on a holiday weekend. It was not fun. It was espeshully not fun for Mr Tasty Face and the Food Lady becuz the emerjinsy vet dranes yer peeple's bank akownt win yoo have to go thare. But Mr Tasty Face and the Food Lady didn't mind so much becuz by that time they luvd me vary much, and that it was werth having to eet beens 'n' weeneez for three munths just to be abul to have me arownd. We had to wate menny howrs to see the gerl in the wite kote, and then finely she stuk sumthing up my poophole, and the poop came owt. I felt better. It was the last time I was ever konstipatid in my life. Frum that minit on, I had the sqwerts.

The sqwerts have defined my life. They have cawzed me to have to have my feet washed abowt ten sqwillion times in my life becuz as soon as I poop, I step in it, and the warm gooey poop sqwishes between my toze, and then I run run run and shake my foot and leeve littul stinky brown footprints all over the howse, or I krawl into the peeple bed and put my pawprints on thare pillowkases and then Mr Tasty Face and/or the Food Lady go, "OH SKEEZIX!" and then they trak me down and ketch me and wash my feet. They mite as well be dipping my littul pink feet in karbolik asid becuz I hate hate hate hate hate gitting wet, even if it's just my feet. It's not always just my feet, tho. I werk hard at trying to cuvver up my poop in the litter box reel good, but sumtimes I get too enthooziastik and the poop and litter sprays evryware and I end up with poop all over me, inklooding my face and eers. Win that happens, I know the bath is coming becuz I heer, "OH SKEEZIX!" and then I heer water running in the sink. *(I don't know why they say the water is "running." The water isn't going anyware. It's not even walking fast. It stays in the sink.)*

Thus began my Sqwerts Saga that kontinyooz to this day. Now I'm more careful abowt not letting it git sqwoosht between my toze so I don't git as many footbaths. And it's better than it wuz. Used to be, it was kinda like Hershey's Choklit Serup, but now it's more like a Jello Choklit Pudding Kup. And it duzn't hardly ever go on the walls anymore, just maybe wunce a week, max. I gess it's whut yoo call progress. I've tride evry remedy thare is frum my vet man and frum all my innernet frends. Theeze remedeez hav inklooded:

1. Barfy wite pills
2. Barfy white gooey likwid
3. Barfy likwid that was supozedly "toona flaverd." (It wuzn't.)
4. Flakes on my food
5. Raw food
6. Turkey baby food
7. Cheeze
8. Speshul cat food
9. Speshul dog food (I'm not kidding. Woof.)
10. Metuhmyoosil
11. Powder on my food
12. Fasting with reintrodukshun of allergin-free food (the fasting part lasted almost until lunchtime the ferst day)
13. Rice and white chikkin meet

Some of theeze werked better than others, but none has bin a kompleet kyoor. Anyway, my problim with the sqwerts is how I wun the titul, "The stinkiest kitten ever born." Yoo see, not only do I poop a lot of runny poop, but it has the hi-est consentrayshun of stink partikuls of any substinse that is fownd on planit erth. I kid yoo not.

Anyway, I stayed a runt the rest of my life. I got a littul bigger, but not by much, even tho I eet a lot more evry day than my big bruther Mao does (and Mao cood stand to miss a few meels if yoo git my drift.) So I looked a little forlorn and sikly, even tho I felt okay. That's win the Food Lady desided to start dressing me up. She ubzervd that I hardly ever came owt of my cat bed berrito win it was cold, wich wuz almost alwayz. So she bot me a bloo and gold Cal Bears swetter. At ferst, I wuzn't shur I liked it. I krawld along with my body close to the grownd, looking like one of thoze legless munchkin cats. But then I realized that it kept me warm owtside my bed, and I liked the way it looked on me. It shode off my bloo eyes. The Food Lady isn't a Cal fan, but she thought the blue swetter lookt nice on me. And I lookt vary kuhleejit, wich is how kids hoo go to kollij look. I lernd how to take my bloo and gold Cal Bears swetter off later in the day win it isn't freezing anymore. It werked owt good and I liked being stylish. Evrybuddy hoo sees me akts like they've never seen a cat in a swetter before, and that's becuz I am a trendsetter.

So I started to git more kyoot outfits. And altho bloo was my ferst faverit color, I soon discuverd a new faverit color: PINK! Pink is nice becuz my noze and my pawpads and my ears and all of my skin underneeth my fur is pink. So the Food Lady bot me lots of kyoot pink outfits, and I developt my own yooneek stile. Sumtimes the Food Lady wood make me ware hats. Like, she has this grate foto of me waring a green Saynt Patriks Day hat. But I don't like hats so much bekuz they smoosh down my big ears. It's vary uncumfterbul.

It was abowt that time that I tride to deside whut I wunted to be win I grew up. I wuz a littul loneley becuz I was trapt inside the big howse and they woodn't let me be an owtside cat and I reely wunted to be abul to have fun with other cats. I'm vary owtgoing and soshul. That's win I discuverd the innernet.

The innernet is sumthing that livs inside the big teevees in the Food Lady and Mr Tasty Face's office. It sends messijiz to other cats hoo also have the big teevees in thare peeple's offices. The innernet is vary fun. The Food Lady helped me to figyur owt how to make a blog on the innernet, and I made my ferst blog on March 15th, 2005. I put my pikchur in the green hat in the blog. And I started blogging a fyoo times a week, win I had nooz, or win I was bord. The nice thing abowt blogs is that they don't akshully have to be intresting. Yoo can just rite whutever yoo feel like riting.

The Food Lady helped me git my own domane name (skeezixthecat.com). I wuz reely reely lukky that no one had snapt it up yet! This ment that besides just a blog, I cood have a web site, too. And my own emale adress: skeezix@skeezixthecat.com.

And then sumthing amazing happend. Cats frum the innernet started sending me messijes. I sent them messijes bak. And we bekame frends.

One of the ferst cats to send me a messije was Shabby Cat, hoo wuz reskyood by a vary nice man and ladey and brot to liv with them in thare home. Shabby

Cat is vary byootiful, with vary vary long fur and nice eyelashes.

And then I made frends with Kismet the Big Man Cat. Kismet is a manly man cat hoo is my role modul. He's vary smooooth with the ladeez. Kismet also has good fashun sense, altho he tends to ware greens and bloos and browns insted of pinks. He is ginormus! He's like, 16 pownds, and I am less than haff his size. He used to hang with a gang of chiwawas. I think if we hung owt together, we'd kinda be like the Skipper and Gillygun. (I luv watching Gillygun's Ilund. Jinjer and Missuz Howl have the best outfits!! Jinjer has the boas, and Missuz Howl has the bling. Boy, I cood just watch that show 24 howrs a day!)

And then I bekame frends with Rosie and Cheeto hoo liv in an ixotik place called San Fransisko. Rosie and Cheeto yoost to liv in Myammi. Rosie is sassy, but in a nice way. She's part skunk, with a stripe on her tale, even those she's a tortie and isn't supost to have a stripe on her tale. Cheeto is a vary kool dood and he and Rosie are best frends. They red blogs for a vary long time and left comments, and then finely got thare own blog!

The vary best day of my life happend win I fownd owt that my blog helpt save a sweet kitty frum the sausage faktery. The cat's name was Éclair. Her mom had emaled me saying she'd bin reeding my blog and it started her thinking abowt gitting a cat. She hadn't had a cat in many yeers. She was thinking of gitting a Simeeze. I emaled her bak and gave her sum infermayshun, and a few weeks later she emaled me bak to let me know she'd gone to the pownd and adopted a sweet part-Simeeze littul cat and she named her Éclair. And Éclair started a blog of her own. Yoo can planely see why that was the best day of my life! My eyes were wet, I was so happy!

It wuz abowt this time that I wint to Bullevard Pet Hospital for the big sleep. I didn't mind going as much as I did the ferst time becuz I'd bin thare so many times for my sqwerts that I made lots of frends thare, like Jeeen, and Kathey, and Jessikuh, and Mark and Shon, and they always liked to chek owt my outfits. Before, the Food Lady always stade with me. This time she dropt me off and wint away. I was a-scared. It was kinda kold even tho I was waring my Skeezix the Cat tee shert, and I shivverd. I thot maybe I'd bin a bad boy for being too stinky and poopy and ugly and they were gitting rid of me and sending me to the sausage faktery.

The man in the bloo kote took me in a room and torcherd me with needuls, and I wint to sleep. It was a vary vary deep sleep, not like the catnaps I uzhully take. Win I woke up, I wuz kinda woozy, and my goodie sak wuz sore. I likkt it and likkt it. Still sore. Likking didn't help. But amazingly, I saw that my big bruther Mao was in the kayje next to me. He sed he thot he wuz thare to have his teeth kleend. That made me werry. Maybe the Food Lady and Mr Tasty Face had desided to git rid of Mao, too, for not brushing his teeth more offin and gitting stinky breth!

Well, at leest we were being sent off to the sausage faktery together. I didn't werry too much more abowt it becuz I was vary vary sleepy like Dorthy and the Kowerdly Lion in the feeld of popeez and I coodn't hold my eyes open any longer and I wint bak to sleep. I dreemd I was in the Wizzerd of Oz moovey, wich is one of my faverit mooveys becuz I LOVE Glinda the good witch's nice pink outfit and tiara, and I love Dorthy's roobey slippers, too! (Altho I don't akshully ware slippers myself.)

Win I woke up, I was in the bloo prizzin box and the Food Lady was talking to me. Then I wint bak to sleep and woke up at my howse. Mao wuz with me. I'm not shur whut had happend during that day, iksept that afterwerd, I didn't wunt to play my faverit game anymore ware Mao iz my gerlfrend and I clime on his bak and put the bitey on his nek. And my nice big wite goodie sack was smaller. My frends Sammy and Miles call it a hoo-ha-ectomy. I gess that's the teknikul term for it.

Then my days started to git vary bizzy. After brekfist, I like to play. Mostly, I play with myself. My faverit toy is my tinsel wand. I also love my Whirly*Pop kardbord Klubhowse and my Village Market brown bag and my string. Then after playing I have to do my blogging. Then I have to do patrols, ware I trot thru the howse making shur that evrything is okay and thare are no introoders. This is a vary importunt job, and I take it vary seriusly. And I have to spend part of my day shopping for kyoot outfits on the innernet. To pay for my kyoot outfits, I opend a store ware peeple cood buy Skeezix merchundise like tee-sherts and greeting cards and koffey mugs. Mao sez it's all a bunch of krap, but I think it's nice stuff. And it all has my pikchur on it!

Anyway, one morning, during my patrol, I saw a cat owt in the bak yard by ware the forest starts hoo was not Mao or Rocky. It was an introoder! Well, this is just the sort of thing I'm supost to be on the lookowt for during my patrols. The cat lookt like a wild jungle cat, all stripey and spotted. I'd never seen a stripey/spotted cat before. I thought maybe this was a wild leperd or tiger frum the forest, like I'd seen in Nashunul Jeografik magazeen. The wild leperd was trying to steel Rocky's leftover brekfist! Well, I began howling at the top of my lungs win I saw that! The Food Lady and Mr Tasty Face came running! The wild leperd cat ran away into the forest, but after a wile he started coming bak evry morning.

Of korse, the Food Lady felt sorry for him becuz he was starving, so she started feeding him win Mr Tasty Face wasn't looking. And grajully, he began to stay longer and not run into the forest win we saw him. The Food Lady talked to him in soft talk, not lowd like she uzhully talks, and she'd git down on her hands and neez so she wuzn't way taller than him. It's not a very flattering vyoo frum the bak, but I think it was less skarey for the wild leperd cat. And she got him yummy food like toona, wich she shared with me and my big bruther Mao. And after a long time she got the wild leperd cat to let her tuch him. And evenchully, he wasn't a-skared any more. Wich was not such a good thing becuz he was not only an introoder and a wild leperd but he was also a psyko-kitty hoo skracht and bited people sumtimes. And he wood walk rite under the peeple's feet to rub aginst thare legs and trip them. That's how he got his name Tripper. They calld him Trip for short becuz it was the name of thare faverit karucter in the teevee show "Enterprise."

Soon after Trip got used to being tucht by the Food Lady, one morning she put him in the kardbord prizzin box and took him away in the bloo masheen. That made me sad becuz I thot maybe he and me cood be frends. My big bruther Mao and Rocky the Gutter Cat are geezers, not kittins like me, so I didn't reely have anywun to play with. Tripper lookt like he mite want to play with me becuz we sorta played thru the skreen on the dek evry nite, and I hoped we cood become rassling buddies. So I wuz upset win the Food Lady took him away in the bloo masheen becuz he was going to the sausage faktery and I wood never see him agin.

But she brot him bak that nite! Turns owt, she just took him to the vet man to have that thing done to his goodie sak, just like she did with me! (Whut's with it with her and the goodie saks? Mr Tasty Face better watch owt!) She told Mr Tasty Face that the hoo-ha-ectomy and all Tripper's shots and tests and stuff cost as much as 1163 cans of Fancy Feest Sliced Turkey in Gravy. I wuz werried that that wood meen I wood have to eet less to pay for Trip's hoo-ha-ectomy, but it didn't seem to matter. I still got to eet as much as I wunted. Anyway, that's win Tripper kind of bekame a member of owr famly. He livs owtside becuz of the psyko kitty thing, but he has a heeted cat bed and his life is a lot better and he gits to come inside the howse sumtimes for short supervizd vizits. They still don't let him play with me, tho, bekuz he (like evry cat) is twice my size, and, well, he's psyko.

The other introoders I have to werry abowt are the vishus deer. Shur, now *evrybuddy* knoze abowt the vishus deer thret, but it was *me* hoo ferst told the innernets all abowt it and spred the werd. Yoo see, the vishus deer liv in the forest by my howse. Mao and Rocky told me that at nite, the vishus deer wander the streets of owr nayburhood, looking for tender, joosy yung cats to eet. They have ginormous horns wich they use to skewer the tender yung cats they want to eet. Yoo can see them poking thare nozes into rozebushes and the other flowers in owr frunt yard, and ripping apart anything that the cats mite be hiding in. PLUS, my best frend Victor Tabbycat got a terrifying foto of the vishus deer's lazer beem eyes! His vary brave hyooman saw a vishus deer at nite and took a pikchur with a speshul flashy thing on the camra. It was purrfikt for reeveeling the eerie glow of the vishus deer's lazer beem eyes! At nitetime, the vishus deer use thare lazer beem eyes to blind the tender yung cats so that the cats are defenseless aginst them, and they can skewer the poor cats more eezily. I make shur the vishus deer don't come in owr howse, and although that's a hard thing to do, so far I've bin suksessful. Not one singul vishus deer has bin in owr howse sinse I came to liv in Castro Valley by the big forest.

Wunce I understood the gravitey of the vishus deer thret, I made it my mishun to inkreese awareniss of it in the online cat comyoonity by distribyooting FSAs (Feline Servise Annownsmints) in my blog. Amazingly, sum cats had NO IDEEYA how danjerus the vishus deer can be. Yet for many of them, the vishus deer are lerking in the forests neer thare homes, just wating to catch the cats off-gard and stab them with thare horns and eet them. I did a lot of innernet reeserch on the vishus deer and fownd terrifying fotos of innosint cats with vishus deer just momints before they got skewerd. It's kind of like win people watch the moovey, "Red Asfalt" in driver's train-ing. It makes yoo a littul sik to yer stumik, but it reely hits home whut can happin if yer not vijilunt. So if yoo google "vishus deer," yoo'll how EVRYWUN knows abowt them now. I think I mite evin git a No-bell prize for my werk in this area.

Now Mao and Rocky know ferst-hand how seerius the vishus deer thret is. Mao hides under one of the bloo masheens and Rocky runs like a gerl far far away winever they spot a gang of vishus deer maurodding thru owr nayburhood. So I'm vary prowd to say that they invented the paten-pending "Mao & Rocky's Vishus Deer Repelunt™," and they sell it on the innernet. It's bin a littul slow to take off, but I bet they'll become rich millyunairs one day frum this ontreprenuriul venchur. I keep telling them they need to make an informershul, but Mao duzn't like being on camra becuz he sez the camra adds ten pownds, and he's gitting a littul chunky.

Now the vishus deer are pritty much owtside creechurs, and I liv inside. I'm an inside cat becuz I reely don't have hare on my ears, and I'd git sunbernd if I wint owtside, and I'm such a runt that big berds like owls and hoks and stuff hoo liv in the big forest wood luv to swoop down on me and skyooer me with thare taluns and eet me for dinner. That duzn't sownd fun. The forest is filld with all kinds of danjerus creechurs like:

1. Vishus deer
2. Vishus aardvarks
3. Vishus jackelopes
4. Vishus sqwerls
5. Vishus buneez
6. Vishus giant wild turkeez
7. Kiyoh-teez (I don't know if thare vishus or not, I just heer them go wooooo woooooo woooooo in the nite.)

So as yoo can planely see, going owtside is like playing rushin roolett.

Mao and Rocky hav told me thay'll teech me thare speshul ninja moovs if I pay them $100, but I came to realize the peeple will never let me go owtside alone anyway, so thare's reely no point. I did try to make a brake for it and eskape on my own a cuppul of times. Once I got way far away, in the forest behind the howse next to owrs. But I soon realized that I was owt of my element and then I herd vishus deer coming thru the shrubery to eet me. And I was cold becuz I wuzn't waring a kyoot outfit. I started yelling at the top of my lungs (wich isn't that lowd becuz my voice is kinda high and sqweeky). Then I realized that I shoodn't be advertizing to the vishus deer ware I was hiding. I stopped for a moment and held my breth. I was sertin that the end was neer. My life flasht before me. Sudenly, bersting thru the shrubery was the Food Lady! I was never so happy to see her! She sayvd me frum sertin deth! I jumpt in her arms and purrd until I was ikzawsted.

So the peeple got me a harniss. A harniss looks like whut they hang criminuls with. It goze arownd my chest and nek like a noos, and then it attaches to a ropey thing that Mr Tasty Face holds. I can go for walks owtside win I'm waring my harniss, and I'm pritty safe becuz Mr Tasty Face is rite thare with me. The problem with the harniss is that I don't go far becuz I stop and snif evry singul thing I go by, espeshully pee spots. And thare are LOTS of pee spots. So I don't git to see much, but I snif a lot. That's win the Food Lady desided I needed a stroller, cuz the sniffing part drives her insane. She'll git ikzasperated and say lowd, "SKEEZIX! Do yoo hav to snif EVry. SINGul. THING????" (I put the periods in becuz win she sez this, she pawziz and sez eech werd like it's in its own sentinse, just like the grate Captin James T Kirk duz in my faverit teevee show, Star Trek.)

So we did sum shopping on the innernet, and orderd a Jeep Rubicon™ Pet Stroler.

The stroler is the best invenshun in the histery of the werld. I luvd it frum the minit I saw it. Unforchewnitly, it is not pink (my faverit color), but otherwize it is purrfikt. It has big rubber offrode tires becuz it is a Jeep Rubicon Pet Stroler and Jeep Rubicons are offrode veehikuls. It has a cup holder and a shelf ware I can keep a change of clothes and an extra swetter, and it even has brakes. I sit inside and can look at the werld go by frum one of the 4 windows it has. It's reely grate. My stray cat frend Trip follows us winever I go owt in my Jeep Rubicon Pet Stroler. In fakt, I made a moovey of that, called "The Pink Panther Rides Agin." (I'm the pink panther.) I think Trip wunts a stroler of his own. My big bruther Mao and Rocky think it's the stoopidest invenshun in the histery of the werld and they won't go neer it. So it's just mine mine mine. Wich is better any-way.

On the innernet, I met a lot of other cats hoo have strolers. We talk abowt owr stroles and win I had my berthday party, sum of them gave me stuff to pimp my stroler with, inclooding a lisinse plate and pink hangy downy things and byootiful patches frum Purple Moon and stuff like that. So it's a groovin' ride.

And I rote abowt my Jeep Rubicon stroler on my blog, and other cats got them, too! My best frend Kaze (hoo is ikzaktly like me – a big-eared Oriental with a meezer big bruther) got one, but she yells like she's being torcherd win she rides in it, so I think only her bruthers go for rides now. My best frend Kalin got one, too! My best frend Rocky Ann has the most pimped owt stroler EVER, with lots of peece sines on it and TROLLS on the frunt! Rocky Ann also loves PINK and has a pink Hello Kitty bedroom all to herself, and even has Hello Kitty pajamas! The Food Lady is not shoor she wants to pimp owt my stroler much more becuz then Mr Tasty Face won't push it or wunt to be seen within 5 miles of it. I don't understand that, becuz the stroler wood be so byootiful, I wood think Mr Tasty Face wood be prowd to show it off! Sumtimes I don't understand him!

Anyway, cats liked to vizit my blog to see my kyoot outfits and lern importunt stuff like abowt the vishus deer, so it wuzn't long before I bekame an innernet sellebrity. I made a moovey with my best frend, Samuel L Jackson, named, "Skeezix on a Plane." That got me intristed in durekting and prudoosing mooveys. One of my ferst efferts was, "Mr Tasty Face's Tasty Face." It was a runaway hit and got over 300 hits on youtube. I was hookt. Next I made, "The Adventures of Rocky the Gutter Cat," and, "The Birds," and "Mr Sqwerl Comes to Visit," and the stroler moovey I told yoo abowt, "The Pink Panther Rides Agin." They were all kritikul and popyooler suksesses.

Suddenly I fownd myself with lots of frends. But they were all good, sinseer frends, not sikofants and hangers-on, like whut hang with Purris Hilton and Linsey Lohan. I joined MySpace, but I got too many invitayshuns frum kollij gerls with webcams. Then I fownd Catster, wich is like MySpace for cats, only not skanky. I started a groop called "Frends of Skeezix (FOS)" on Catster. This was so I cood have my berthday party thare. For my berthday party, I maled owt party paks to all my frends that had toys and treets and nip and FOS swag in them. I reely just wunted to make shur evrywun had stuff to party down with on the day of my berthday, but I was shokt win I started gitting kards and pakijes in the male. The man in the bloo shorts hoo brings my male was imprest! Evry singul day he brot pakij after pakij. Even my big bruther Mao was a littul imprest. He'd bin kind of a poop-hed and was meen and sed that all my innernet frends were imajinery frends until he saw all the toys and catnip I got in the male. Then he chanjed his toon and asked me if he cood share sum of it. Of korse, I shared evrything with him even tho he'd bin a poop-hed becuz he's the best big bruther I ever had.

My secund berthday party was held on Catster, and I made a moovey of it, too. Lots and lots and lots of cats came. We had a grate time. Rocky the Gutter Cat was the bartendur, and since Rocky had bin having sum pee problms, Trip bakt him up behind the bar. They also had a table of Temptayshun, with Temptayshuns treets, and a nip bar, too. Rocky werked very hard to put together a speshul bar menu with drinks he invented just for my party. Heer are the speshulty drinks frum Rocky's Bar the way Rocky rote them on the speshul bar menu for the party:

BEER
frum the fameus Fat Cat Brewery (fatcatbrewery.com). I've desided to serv thare "Old Bad Cat Barley Wine Ale" at the party. I've ordered a hundred kegs. That sownded like enuf for a hundred kitties.

THE ROCKATINI
Combines toona joose and fresh devon creem, with an anchovey on top and a catnip sprig as garnish. They are, of korse, shaken, not stird.

CATNIP WINE
A popyler staple.

CATNIP KOOLERS
Combins catnip wine, sum bubbley and a spritz of toona joose on top.

CATMINT JULEP
Lots and lots of catmint with a speshul blend of sekrit ingreedients. Yoo folks frum the south shood like theze.

CATARITA
This south of the border faverit combines a chilled chikkin broth, likker and catnip. It's blended with ice so it's kool and refreshing.

CATAPOLITAN
Like a Rockatini, only pink.

THE VISHUS DEER
It starts with ten parts Jaegermeister (wich is hella strong likker), then it gits blended with a pawfull of Natural Balance Venison & Pees cat fud, a spritz of catnip essense, creem and some ice topped with a blast of Tabasko!

They served regyuler drinks, too, but most evrywun pikt sumthing frum Rocky's speshul menu. The Vishus Deer was the most popyooler drink. Sum of the cats got reely likkerd up. Grover volunteerd his baby bruther Dexter to be the litter box attendint, but Dexter drank too many Vishus Deers and then he blew chunks and past owt in one of the litter boxes and the litter got wet and caked on haff his face: whut a mess!

We playd a reely fun game called "Pin the Tale on the Maobutt." It was like pin the tale on the donkey, but with Mao insted of a donkey. Mao was a littul kranky abowt that and thretend to soo, but I kalmd him down by promising him he'd meet lots of hot gerl cats at the party. And thare were LOTS of hot gerl cats like Rosie and Bonnie Underfoot and Jasmine and Chloe and Sanjee and Gimme's sister Ele', and Sadie (hoo looks IKZAKTLY like Rocky) and Princess Zippy and Kalin and Brandi and Mrs B and Midnight and Cocoa and Bathsheba and Rasta (hoo wore an amazing ranebow 'fro wig) and Boni Maroni and – well, shoot, I know I'm gonna leeve sumwun owt, but I can't keep listing all the hot gerl cat names or else yoo'll git bord.

Anyway, we had a Party Hat contest, wich Cocoa and Lucky Boo won, and a Werd Serch Contest, wich Bubbles wun, and a Trivia/Skavenjer Hunt Contest, wich Bravely Sir Robin wun. Sanjee kist me and I got so flusterd, I wet my pants. Evrybuddy was dancin, and playin, and doin nip and drinkin and blowin chunks: it was a very suksessful party! I opend my prezints, and got lots and lots of pink stuff and toys and nip and 2 fether boas (one to ware; one to eet), and a New York Yankees cap frum my best frend Jeter Harris. Afterwerd, I made a moovey of it wich was anuther big youtube hit with over 120 vyooings!

After the party, I rote thank yoo notes to evrywun becuz the Food Lady sez it's pawlite. It took a very very long time becuz I got many cards and gifts, and I had to rite them in longhand wich, as yoo know, takes furrever.

I think my handriting cood use sum improovmint, so it's going to be one of my new yeer's rezolushuns next yeer.

The next event I pland was a Halloween Costoom Kontest. It got more than 50 entreez. That's a lot! My best frend Nitro drest up as ME for Halloween wich just made me laff and laff. He wore a pink shert and a berthday hat ikzaktly like my berthday hat, and a Frend of Skeezix buttun and hyooje pink ears! It was the gratest! My best frend Kismet the big man cat drest up as Elvis, and Kismet werked hard pozing with kind of a curly snarly lip just like Elvis. He probly got all the gerl cat votes. And Tiggy drest up as a Playboy Bunney kompleet with big pom poms in frunt, becuz Kismet wares a Hugh Hefner robe (win he's not drest like Elvis) and she has the hots for Kismet. So yoo can planely see that it was a grate kontest!

And since I was now offishully a big boy, I got a job. Yoo see, FilmLoop.com had shone my blog on thare web site as an ikzampul of grate blogs uzing FilmLoop. So win they were developing the next vershun of thare produkt, they emaled me with an invitayshun to be a beta tester. And I sed yes! So I got a job testing thare produkt for yoozability and then emaling FilmLoop bak with my findings. I think it mite be a springbord to a lukrativ job in the innernet industrey!

So that's the storey of my life so far. It just prooves that even if yer the ugliest, stinkiest cat in the werld like me, yoo can still git lots of frends on the innernet.

Some Conversations With Cats

My Mousie Story
by Max (at 2 years old)

Mom doesn't want me to tell you this, 'cause she's embarrassed about it, but I'm proud that I got an A+ in "Mousing Ability", so I'm telling my story anyway!

All the time I've lived in our house, and even before that my brother George says, sometimes we get mousies. I think they're great, but Mom says they have something called "diseases" and doesn't want them around. She's always afraid we'll get sick or something.

Anyway, I get the mousies and when I'm done with them, I just leave them where they are and go play with something else. But here's where my story gets good.

Mom was leaving to go out and saw one of my dead mousies in the living room. She made a sound something like this. "AAAAIIEEEE, where are these (swear) things coming from??!!" Then she got this blue thing called a dustpan and a long broom. She held the broom way out in front of her and poked the mousie to be sure it was dead. Of course it was dead! A guy with my mousing skills would never leave a live mousie running around!

Then she scrinched up her nose, broomed the mousie onto the dustpan and held it down tight. We all followed her to see where she was going with it. Maybe she would show my mousie to Dad!! But she took it into the bathroom and flushed it away.

I heard Mom say to Dad maybe they should call the Governor of Catifornia to…

MOM Wait .. Arnold Schwarzenegger?
MAX Yeah, you know, The Terminator.
MOM No Max, that's EX-terminator.
MAX Whatever. MY mousies would be gone either way!

Things I Know About Christmas
by Max (at 18 months old)

I was too young to remember last Christmas, so I looked at TV and asked my sister Tipper & my brother George about it. For the rest of you who are too young too to know about it, this is what I found out.

See, there's this guy called Santa that brings toys and stuff to all good kitties and he's fat 'cause he eats too many treats. I might leave a few of mine out for him but I'm telling Mom to hide the rest so he doesn't eat them all.

Santa has long, white whiskers like me, but he wears red jammies with bells on them. When he isn't busy making toys he hangs out where it snows forever and drinks Coke with polar bears. He talks to deers that have flashy, red light bulbs for noses. I know what deers are, 'cause I've seen them in my yard, but I'm pretty sure none of them had light bulbs.

And get this…his carrier can fly! It's magic and can go all around the world. We have a carrier too, but we don't fly to the V.E.T. We go in the car.

Sometimes Santa stands out in the cold by stores and rings bells and gets money to help everybody. Mom says this is a good thing and she gives him some money. Then Santa might hold some leaves over your head and try to kiss you. I'm not sure I like this part 'cause Mom is the only one I let kiss me but maybe I should let Santa kiss me too, if I want any toys!

Santa has a bunch of helper guys called elves, with sparkly skin and they help make all the toys. They wear green clothes and have pointy ears and they look like space aliens from some planet called North Pole. You can send mail to their planet saying how good you are and the elves will read it. Then after they read your mail, the elves give Santa a list of all kitties names to check if they've been "naughty" or "nice" and he checks it twice before his carrier takes off. I know all my friends names will be on his "nice" kitty list.

When Santa comes to your house, his carrier lands on your roof and then Santa falls down the chimney into your fireplace, just like a birdie did in ours. If you don't have a fireplace, I think he probably comes in the same holes that bugs and mousies do. So, if you see a guy in red jammies walking in your house at night, it's OK, he's not a robber. It's just Santa, and he leaves stuff for you by your Christmas tree. Mom says we might not have a Christmas tree this year 'cause she's afraid we'd knock it over. Wait ... if we don't have a tree, where will Santa leave our toys?

So anyway, if you've been a "nice" kitty all year, Santa will bring you things. If you've been "naughty", you might get a bag of rocks or maybe NOTHING!

We've been really good, except for maybe just a few times. I want a new cat perch and some new glitter balls to replace the ones we lost under the furniture, and maybe a feather that flies.

Another One Bites The Dust
by Tipper (at 3 years old)

MOM Tipper! What happened to the plant that was in this pot?

TIPPER Um…hmmm…. (looks around)… oh, you mean *that* plant. Well, I…uhhhh…I'm not sure…and, uh…WHY ARE YOU ACCUSING ME, anyway? There are other cats named Tipper, you know!

MOM Yes, but they don't live in this house.

TIPPER Oh yes, good point. Well, then…uh…let me think. Hmmm…let's see…I might have been sitting on the ledge next to flower pot…(yes, that's sounds good)…and uh…yes, it's all coming back to me now. OK…I was sitting there…INNOCENTLY, of course…minding my own business, when um…uhh…all of a sudden, umm…to my complete surprise...uhhh...(oh, I've got it now)... the plant jumped right out of the pot...(yes, that's it!)...all by itself...and it fell on the floor. And I had absolutely nothing to do with it! Yes...as I recall...that's exactly the way it happened.

MOM But how did those bite marks get on the leaves?

TIPPER Bite marks? Uhhh...(looks at clock) Gosh, would you look at the time! Sorry Mom, I'd love to stay and chat, but I've got to run...busy, busy, busy!

Things I Know About The Rainbow Bridge
by George (at 9 years)

I asked Mom about the Rainbow Bridge place where my sister Gracie is now and she said that lots of kitties and other animals there, too. There were 3 other kitties that lived here before us that all went there already.

This is what I know now about the Rainbow Bridge place. It sounds OK to me and Mom told me when it's my turn to go there, even though they will miss me very much, I shouldn't be afraid.

For everyone who has lost a cat recently, I hope this information helps you feel better about the Rainbow Bridge.

· Everyone feels great and no one is sick or hurt or has to take medicine

· There is lots of food and treats and you can eat everything you want

· You never throw up

· There are all kinds of toys and no one tries to take the one you want

· There are enough pillows, blankets and soft places for everyone to sleep on

· It's always warm & sunny - never cold, raining or snowing

· There are plenty of birdies, chipmunks, squirrels and mousies to watch

· Even though there are dogs there, they don't bark at you or chase you

· There's lots of boxes, bags and strings to play with

· There is a mountain of catnip

· There are no V.E.T's to poke you

· There are no carriers you have to be in

· The litterbox is always clean

· You can do anything you want and nobody says "Get off", " Get down" or "Get out of the way"

· You can go anywhere you want, even if you weren't ever allowed outside before

· You **will** see your friends and family again

My Sister's Shower
by Misty (at 4 months)

MISTY I heard something today that I don't understand. On Sunday my human sister is coming to my house to take a shower and Mom says I have to be good. Why? Why should I have to be good while my sister takes a shower?

TIPPER (sigh) Well, I'm the one that asked for a baby sister! OK, now listen Misty, let me explain this. When a lady gets married...

MISTY What's married?

TIPPER Married is when two people love each other and decide they want to be a family, like Mom & Dad.

Anyway, before they get married, the lady gets a shower, but not the kind in the bathtub. It's a special party where everyone gives her presents...sort of like a purrthday or when Santa comes. Oh wait, you don't know about Santa yet do you...and you haven't had a purrthday yet. Hmmm...do you even know what a present is?

OK, let me try this again.

When people get married, they need things for their house, like towels and dishes and stuff. These things are called presents. Then all their friends and family decide to have a party where they give them the presents. A shower party is where everyone comes over and they eat lots of food and cake and they talk and play games. But don't worry we'll put our toys away so no one plays with them.

Then after the people open all their presents, the shower is over and they live happily ever after! Now do you understand?

MISTY Yeah, but I still don't know why I have to be good!

Explaining The Hoo-Ha-Ectomy
by George (at 9 years)

As one of the elders in our cat community, and for the benefit of the younger guys, I feel I must take this opportunity to have a discussion of just what the word "Hoo-ha-ectomy" means. Since this is "G" rated I will be discreet, but in order not to offend any young ladies out there, you girls might want to stop reading here and go take a short nap or watch some birdies.

OK guys, the main reason this is done is so that we can't make kittens and you don't need to be afraid to have it done. You might hear it referred to as "Being fixed or neutered", "Getting clipped" or "Having your bits re-moved", and most of us have experienced our hoo-ha-ectomy early in our lives. My brother Max and I had ours as very young kittens since the shelters we were adopted from wouldn't let us go home without going to the V.E.T. first. The actual procedure is not as bad as being put in the carrier and going in the car, which most of us don't like. Once you get to the V.E.T. you take a short nap and when you wake up, your hoo-has are gone! You might be a little sensitive in that area for a day or two, but in most cases, there are no problems after that.

There are many benefits to us guys in having this done, and I will talk briefly about each of them

Population control – We all know there are too many unwanted kittens that get sent to the Rainbow Bridge without ever finding forever homes. This is a very sad situation. Instead of acting like.... dare I say it....(*whispers*) sex crazed maniacs roaming or "tomcatting" around looking for females, guys without hoo-has can appreciate the ladies for an elegantly curved whisker, a soft meow and a beautiful coat while maintaining a strictly platonic relationship. Plus you have the assurance of not having to pay kitten support or having false paternity claims made against you.

Aggression control - Hoo-ha removal helps you stay calm and relaxed and not go around picking fights with other cats. We are all incredibly handsome guys and want to stay that way, so it's best to avoid fighting.

Weight – Some think that guys without hoo-has will gain weight. Speaking from personal experience, Max and I have not had a problem with this. We maintain our manly physiques at 12 – 16 lb. By controlling your diet and getting enough exercise, you should have no problems either.

Spraying – Also called territorial marking, this is done by guys who still have hoo-has. No gentlemen cat would ever spray and Max and I always use our litter box. Your housemates will appreciate your good manners.

Disease – You can't get cancer of the hoo-has if you don't have them

Safety – You will be happy living indoors or going

out only with supervision. It will keep you safe from harm.

Well, I think that pretty much covers the main points so (*calls out*) all you ladies can come back in the room now. Aha, I knew it! You were there the whole time. Heh, heh, heh.

Being A House Lady
by Misty (at 7 months old)

MISTY I'm seven months old!! YAY!! Since I'm almost grown up now, I decided maybe I should start learning how to be a House Lady. So I followed...

MOM Wait a second. What's a House Lady?

MISTY They take care of the house.

MOM Oh, you mean The Lady of the House.

MISTY That's what I **said**, isn't it? Anyway, I followed Mom around and this is what I learned. For the girls that want to be a House Lady, you have to learn to do ALL these things...IN ONE DAY...and you'll probably be really tired after. It's OK to take a nap like I did.

· *Changing the sheets.* Usually Max helps with this, but he let me do it this time. Take the sheets off the big bed and carry them to the clothes cleaner machine. Then take clean sheets from the closet but before you lay them down and smooth them out, you jump around. It's a good idea to jump on the pillows too.

· *Doing the laundry.* Stinky clothes go in the washer machine and wet clothes come out. Then the wet clothes go in the dryer machine and go around. Before the wet clothes go in, you have to get inside to be sure it's empty, but don't stay in there or you'll go around too! When the clothes come out of the dryer machine, they're all warm, they don't smell stinky anymore and are nice to lay on. Take each thing and fold it flat. Make a high stack that can be knocked over. Pick up the stacks, carry them into the bedroom and put everything on the cedar chest. When the stacks get really high, put some things in drawers.

· *Cleaning the bathroom.* Put some blue stuff in the water and brush it around. Don't drink that water...it's icky! Stand in the bathtub with the spray bottle and make it go skwidg, skwidg, skwidg. Then scrub the glass doors until the dirt is gone. If the scrubber thing accidentally flies out of the tub, don't let it hit you 'cause it smells like the spray bottle. Take the scrubber thing and wash the sink. The paper towel you use to wipe the mirror is good to chase.

· *Dusting.* Take the long hose and put a brush on the end of it, then go whoosh, whoosh on all the furniture. Make the dust go away, but if you see a spider in the corner, don't make it go away. It's OK to eat it.

· *Cleaning the floors.* There's a lot of cat hair around, 'specially on the carpet where Max and I wrestle...plus parts of things that I've torn up like papers and feather toys and things I find in wastebaskets. Take the long hose in all the rooms and make the mess go away. Then take the mop and wash the kitchen floor. A wet floor is good for sliding on and I can go all the way across the kitchen!

· *Going to the store.* I wasn't allowed to go with, but I think this is where Mom gets things we need and then brings them home in bags. Bags are great to look in…you never know what you'll find in there. After you look at everything then you help decide where to put things away. Make sure there's room for things and get in the cabinets to look around.

· *Taking a break.* Sit on the couch and say "Oh, my back!" then put you feet on the table. This is the time to have a snack and look at a magazine. I took a small nap so I could be ready for the next work.

· *Clean the litterboxes.* Scoop out all the stuff in the litterbox that's in the closet. Then put in new litter. Do the same thing with the litterbox in the basement. If the boxes smell really stinky, get a plastic bag and empty everything. Then wash the box. If you have to go, you have to wait until the box is on the floor again. It's OK to tell Mom to hurry up if you have to go really bad.

· *Paying bills.* Take the papers from the box outside, then sit down and look at each one. Say "Why is everything so expensive!" and say some swears. Decide to throw some papers out. These are the ones you're allowed to play with. Later get your purse and some papers and write with a pen. Every time Mom puts the pen down, knock it on the floor.

· *Cooking.* This is for food that Mom & Dad eat. Our food doesn't need to be cooked…it comes in a bag, except for when we have tuna water. It's not good to jump up on the stove top when Mom is standing by it 'cause it freaks her out and she hollers at you! When the food is on a plate though, you can help yourself to what you want.

Sugar
craziequeen

Sugar was a cat. Nothing special, just a black cat with large green eyes that peered out from under shaggy eyebrows. She was lying in the long grass in the sweltering heat, too feeble to move and meowing pitifully at anyone who passed as if crying out for help. How long she had lain there with selfish, thoughtless humans passing her by was not known. She occasionally lifted herself onto her front paws as if trying to get up and free herself from her torment.

I met Sugar on my way from work and fell in love with her at first glance. Her green eyes seemed to be begging me to help her, and she was crying in pain. My heart turned over as I bent down to stroke her. Her fur was matted and underneath the sorry black coat I could feel every rib and count every vertebra. She was just skin and bone and as I moved my hands gently down her flanks I, in my innocence, concluded that she must have been a female cat and heavily pregnant. I could feel no movement in her swollen belly and surmised that no kittens could have survived the torture that had taken its toll on that young body.

I was torn in two. I could not possibly leave the cat in such pain, but perhaps she had an owner who was looking for her at that very moment. I ran my hand over her flanks one more time and made up my mind. She was badly emaciated and very pregnant and it was fairly obvious that nobody cared about her. I gently lifted her and carefully carried her home, and as I walked I murmured gentle words of comfort to ease the cat's distress. She laid her head on my shoulder and, although she gave the odd pained cry, I could tell she was grateful as she attempted to purr.

Once home I gave her a saucer of milk from which she only took a couple sips before settling down on an old blanket I had found and watching me, ears pricked – well, as pricked as she could manage. Now that she was relaxed and fairly comfortable with sustenance within easy reach I could think out my next move. Not much thinking was required to pick up the phone and ring the person who would give the best advice - my mother.

She advised I should ring a vet to get the cat checked over and do whatever was necessary. The first vet that I picked out of the book was very understanding and told me to bring the cat straight in. I called a taxi and prepared a box. The little cat watched me and I looked into her green eyes – oh, such trusting eyes – and then picked her up and laid her in the box, stroking her and letting her know that I cared and that, in her moment of need, someone was there to help her.

After what, in the cat's mind, must have been a hellish ten minutes in the taxi we arrived at the surgery and the vet was as good as her word and saw her immediately.

The vet had very bad news for me. The cat was not female at all, but a tomcat. He was about two years old and a fine looking cat, who unfortunately was dying a long and painful death. He had a fatal case of FIP, Feline Intestinal Peritonitis, which would kill him soon and in great pain. Euthanasia seemed to be the only answer to ease his agony. I checked that I could not help him by taking him home and nursing him back to health. The vet said the disease was too advanced and nothing could be done to cure him.

With a heavy heart I signed the consent form and then I kissed the cat. As I stroked him, he lay down as if he knew what was coming and he welcomed that peace that death would bring to his pain-wracked body and troubled mind. He looked trustingly up into my eyes and I could have sworn he was thanking me. I kept stroking him; not wanting to leave him, although I knew it was best for him. I looked deep into his eyes and then I knew I was glad that I had not left him to suffer alone, and that he had known love and trust before he passed to that better place where he was assuredly bound. I had no doubt that a place would be reserved in Heaven for him, he was such a loving cat and had missed out on so much love in return.

I knew I had to leave him and the vet was so kind. She sympathised with me and let me stay a while to make up to the little cat all the love he had missed out on. Then I tore myself away from those love-filled eyes and opened the door. A thought occurred to me and I turned back to the vet.

"By the way, his name is Sugar. I called him Sugar and he seems to like it."

The vet smiled and nodded, I closed the door on Sugar and went home.

'And now these three things remain;
faith, hope and love. But the
greatest of these is love.'

                    1 Cor 13:13

Gray Cat

In the afternoon
stretching to catch the last rays
warming raw silk fur

no name cat keeps watch
comings, goings, few do note
he catalogues all

Cold weather rolls in
Will anyone notice if

                                        ~Katrina Lovett

Lessons From A Furball
K.A. Thompson

Dusty was 13 years old, and had severe heart, lung, kidney, and liver problems. She took several drugs three times each day, and only hid under the bed when the thought of yet another pill being shoved into her mouth was overwhelming. Most of the time she was quiet; when she felt good, she was alert and spent long lengths of time sitting on top of a box near the bedroom window, staring outside, feeling the breeze through the screen, as she soaked in every detail that she could. With each day that passed it was increasingly obvious that she understood, on some level, that not all was right in her little world, and that she had to take it all in while she could, before her heart gave out.

During one of her last visits with an internal medicine specialist, she stood silently on the exam table, staring out the window with a quiet dignity that was almost eerie. She ignored the conversation behind her, although she certainly could sense it was about her. She was living in the moment, enjoying the world on the other side of the glass. In years past she became excited and agitated—

chittering and dancing in place—anytime she saw a bird close by through a window, but that day she watched with quiet interest as the birds pecked at flowers and stared back at her through the pane of glass. Her breathing, which of late had been more than double what it should have been, eased and she took very calm, even breaths; lost in the moment, the things which robbed her of her health were of less importance than the joy of simply being alive.

As a kitten, and then young cat, Dusty was very territorial; she would defend what she knew to be hers with the speed and dexterity enjoyed mainly by the young. How intense her defense was depended greatly on the importance of what was at stake: her food, her water, her favorite spot to sleep were at the very top of her list. Her territory, the boundaries of what she knew to be her world, always came behind immediate needs. Birds outside the windows, stray animals, even the postman were concern enough to illicit a response, but rarely enough to trigger a defensive reaction. She'd become excited and vocal, but never physical. As long as she felt safe, she'd remain alert but not terribly reactive; if any of those intrusions ventured into the safety of her world—coming through the front door—she would react with immediate defensive strategies, depending on the size of the threat. Sometimes that meant the baring of claws and teeth, sometimes that meant hiding under the bed.

As she aged and became ill, however, the importance of defending certain things lessened. Her zone of personal comfort expanded considerably in size; things that would have sent her scurrying to a safe spot under the bed before merely piqued her curiosity. If one entered her world through the front door she no longer felt pressed to hide, but rather pressed to investigate; you could touch her things, and even touch her, but she wouldn't become irritated or defensive unless she felt that the living things in her life were potentially in trouble. She would protect the family dog. She would step between The Boy and the cable TV repairman. But her food and water became passing necessities. Any spot could be a comfortable spot to sleep, when sleep was even possible. She would even allow others to watch the world through her window with her, to see what there was to see, and to feel the breeze blowing through the screen.

It became obvious that the things that were once important enough to risk physical injury to protect no longer seemed so valuable to Dusty. As she reached the twilight of her life, she understood something that many people never learn: the things we hold dear to us are sometimes just things, and not always worth the physical effort required to keep them. One way or another, there will be more food, more water, another nice spot to curl up and sleep, or another window from which the world can be observed.

In the human world, Dusty wouldn't have fought someone for her wallet; she would have surrendered her car to the moron demanding it. She seemed to be wrapped in the wisdom that knows the years we have here are too few to bother with inordinate worry about the things that can be replaced. She seemed to sense that life is worth defending and treasuring. Dusty wanted to see it all, as much as she could, and she fought for her own life as much as any person would fight against an assailant they cannot see and do not understand.

We spend so many hours of our lives learning to

fight, to defend ourselves and the people around us; we work hard at making ourselves stronger so that if the time ever comes, we have the advantage and can emerge victorious. Intentionally or not, we also train to defend the things we own: don't take my wallet, don't take my purse, don't take my car or my watch or my designer sneakers. Don't touch my stuff, or I'll have to hurt you.

Think of all the hours you've put in considering, even in fantasy mode, defensive strategy and technique. What you would do if someone tried to take something material that you own. Did you create this plan or envision various scenarios so that you could protect your stuff? Is any of that stuff worth dying over? How many people are injured or killed every year because they were confronted by someone who wanted the things that they had, and refused to just give it up and felt pressed to fight for it?

Fighting for stuff.

Is it worth it?

Dusty died after 14 months of dealing with a heart 5 times its normal size, lungs constantly filled with fluid, and kidneys scarred from the medications she had to take. It was an amazing gift that she lived so long. Every day was a new chance to see the world, to look for what really matters. She showed her family in very subtle ways, that living is a gift to not be taken so lightly, and that the stuff that used to seem important really isn't anything more than nice decorations on the lawn—someone can take those, and you'd miss them for a short time, but in the end, you get over it.

What you don't get over is the ability to live with dignity, and that is what is worth fighting for.

RULES – by Sammy and Miles, The Meezers

Efurry kitty must haf rules for their beans, ofurwise, there would be confushun and lots of yelling. Here are some of the rules we live by:

1. The couch is ours
2. The bed is ours
3. The blankets are all ours
4. All the toys are mine (Sammy)
5. All the nip is mine (Sammy)
6. All the ham is mine (Miles)
7. All smelly stinkies must be deposited in the middle of the night if the litterbox is in the bedroom. This makes for good smell-a-vision dreams for the beans.
8. Beans must remain sitting on the couch until the kitty decides to get off your lap
9. All stinky goodness must be given at exactly the same time (minus 1 minute) each day, until you are forced to get up in the middle of the night to give us breakfast
10. Just open the treat bag and put it on the floor – we will take care of emptying it.
11. Don't leave your shoes out if you don't want to find a hairball in them.
12. Don't leave the human litterbox room door open if you don't want to find fings eifurr in the sink or in the human litterbox

Teamwork
Karen Jo Gray

I once lived in an apartment with a roommate, a cat named Josephine (who claimed me) and a dog named Maurice (who owned my roommate). Josephine and Maurice took to each other almost immediately, though there was a little initial growling and hissing over whose food bowl was whose and whether doggies were allowed to finish up any kitty crunchies left over after dinner. The answer turned out to be yes, as long as I was prepared to get Josephine some more in the middle of the night if she got hungry.

One Saturday, my roommate were both feeling rather lazy about cooking and there wasn't much in the house, so we ordered in a large pizza that would serve for both lunch and dinner. We munched down lunch, amid much hungry stares from Maurice and curiosity from Josephine (who didn't like people food at all, but was always very curious about what anyone was eating). After a while, we went to the grocery store. The leftover pizza was left in the box on top of the refrigerator, as it would not fit inside, high enough to be safe from salivating dogs, or so we thought.

When we returned, there was no kitty in the window, or joyful barks from just inside the door. This was highly unusual. We came into the living room and there on the floor, dragged partway into the hall, was a decidedly ragged-looking pizza box. No cats or dogs were to be seen anywhere. We could only surmise that, being egged on by Maurice, Josephine had jumped up on the counter, then onto the top of the refrigerator (which was something she had never done before, to my knowledge) and pushed down the pizza box. The pair of them somehow got the box open, as evidenced by both cat and dog toothmarks on the cardboard. Maurice then pigged out to his little heart's content and Josephine probably licked a little cheese. When they heard us coming home, both of them went into hiding.

Once we had figured this out, my roommate and I burst out laughing and Josephine and Maurice miraculously reappeared. There was much joyous tail wagging and ankle rubbing. All was well, for who could be mad at such an ingenious pair?

> My mistress is really quite sweet,
> Always good for a pet or a treat,
> But she ran from the room
> And screamed "Get me a broom!"
> When I laid my best mouse at her feet.
>   –Karl Schultz

The Corner in the Basement
Sammy Meezer

There's a corner in the basement that calls to me
Whenever the door is open, I have to run to it
I have to. HE is there.
The One Who Came Before
I know it. I can still smell him there.
I can hear him. He talks to me.
This is the only place I can hear him.
This was his favorite place to play.
The corner in the basement.

He tells me that HE is the reason I am here
He chose me.
He chose me to help Norton with his loneliness for
him
He chose me to help Mommy with her sadness
He chose me so that I would have the love that I
needed.
I tell him that I have more love than I thought was
possible.
I thank him.
I thank him every time I can get there
Every time I can get to the corner in the basement.

The Half-opened Door
Victoria Lyn Ellsworth
(inspired by Cammie)

Nothing has ever
Intrigued a cat more
Than something as simple
As a half-opened door.
Her tail just quivers,
Her whiskers quake,
As she ponders and muses
On the mischief she'll make.
Just what could there be
Behind that door?
Perhaps cobblies or woozlies –
Good Heavens, what more?
Curiosity raised,
She creeps towards the door.
Her body stretched out,
Hugging close to the floor.
She pounces and bats
At the door with her paw.
It swings slowly open,
Can you guess what she saw?
An empty room
Lay behind that door,
A place that she'd left
Only moments before…

Our Lives
Sammy and Miles – The Meezers

It was a day in summer
Wet, scary, so many noises
Why am I here?
Where did my mommy go?
Why can't I find my home?

There's others out here, big and mean
They left something over there that smells good
I'm so hungry
I think I'll stay here – hidden from the others
Oh oh oh someone found me
Wait, he seems nice
Older, wiser, nicer
He's bringing a big thing with him
Up up up I go.
HISS HISS HISS
She's not falling for my tough talk.
Cuddling, I remember this
We're going somewhere – inside
This is not MY inside though

Oh, there's 2 others here – the one who found me
And another. She doesn't like me.
I cower from her.
The big thing wraps me up and cuddles me
I can't help myself PURRRRR PURRRR PURRRR
She gives me yummy food
She rubs my belly
She said she will help me find my mommy if I want
I don't know. Maybe. I tell her we should sleep on it.

I've been here a while now – I guess she never found
my other mommy
That's ok, because I really didn't want to leave.
The other kitties were nice
I get lots of cuddles
And kisses
And TOYS.
I don't think I ever want to leave. – *Sammy Meezer*

It was always warm and comfortable where I was
I had a mommy kitty who loved me
And a sister kitty to play with
The man there was very nice
There was another lady and a younger lady
But they didn't pay too much attention to me

One day, a strange lady came into the warm place
And the man there was telling her about me and my
sister
She picked up my sister and cuddled her
Then the hands came for me

HISSS HISSS HISSS HISSS
NO NO NO
She says I have beautiful eyes
Well, thank you, yes I do
She talks to the man more
And then it's dark
I am being picked up
And taken somewhere
Big metal machine with wheels
HISS HISS HISS
TAKE ME BACK HOME

There's a new warm place
With new brothers and a new sister
One brother is little like me
He looks like me too
He's fun to play with
But the older brother
Who cannot walk well
He is the nicest
I love to cuddle with him in the warm window

We all play during the day
We have good food
And treats
The mommy gives us wonderful cuddles and kisses
We miss the older kitties
They have gone to the Bridge
Even though I missed my other home at first
I don't ever want to leave here – *Miles Meezer*

Along Comes Buddah
Max the PsychoKitty

Buddah Pest stumbled into my world in such a blur that at first I was not sure that I had seen correctly. Surely there was not, as my brain told me in the flicker of a second I had seen it, another kitty inside that little purple box with the wires on it. It couldn't be; it was far too small, just a simple puff of black fur. It looked more like something the vacuum cleaner had hocked up, only more sinister and forbidding.

The People went straight from the front door to the Younger Human's room with the purple box, refusing to allow me the opportunity to investigate properly.

But then the smell hit me.

Kitty.

They had, for sure, allowed another kitty to enter my domain, and given it the space that the Younger Human had begun to occupy only a few months before, the room he had overtaken from the Woman, back when it was an Office and my special napping place. Oh, I didn't mind giving up my special napping place because it meant that the Younger Human was there, and out of all the People, he is my favorite People.

I sat beside the closed door, listening carefully for signs of this other kitty. I knew he was inside that room with it, I knew it as surely as I knew I would not get nearly as much Stinky Goodness for dinner as I would like.

(I would like a full can, but my People are mean and selfish and only allow me half a can. As if a kitty can sustain itself on half a can of Stinky Goodness. They keep saying I'm fat but I know better, because I'm *starving*.)

The Younger Human had a puffy black ball of kitty in his room.

He was cheating on me.

I could scarcely believe the reality that was slowly descending upon me like a wet sack of premium kitty crack. My Younger Human. My special napping place. My home. Mine! They allowed another kitty into MY SPACE.

I sat outside the door, and heard its tiny little meows, and its tiny feet thundering across the floor; I wondered, just for a moment, if there were perhaps 15 kitties in that room, but that puff of black fur was only big enough for one kitty, and barely that. I waited patiently, hoping the door would open and I could get inside to get a better look at this furry little intruder. And to pass the time, I played with my red felt kitty crack toy, the one that's supposed to look like a People candy bar. I'm not dense enough to think that there's actual candy under that red felt, but what the heck, it had some premium nip inside, so I was not about to refuse it.

Batting it back and forth, occasionally rubbing my face on it, I played and waited.

And then it happened.

Then the first of many horrors happened.

A tiny little paw reached from under the door, its claws bared, and it snagged my red felt kitty crack toy.

It took my toy!

"Give it back!" I shouted, to no avail. The Woman had seen it happened, but all she did was laugh and tell me I probably wasn't getting it back.

"Go in there and get it!" I demanded.

No, she said, picking me up and rubbing me under the chin—which normally I would have enjoyed, even if I would not admit that to her—Buddah was sick and they couldn't let me have the toy back, in case whatever he had could make me sick too.

Let me get this straight—I thought it but did not say out loud, because I have learned over the years that the People simply won't take the time to learn to understand me—you not only brought another kitty into MY house, but you brought a SICK kitty in and are going to let it take MY toys and MY Younger Human?

She carried me into the living room and sat in the big comfy chair, still holding onto me. Oh, she explained as if she had really heard my thoughts, they didn't KNOW the kitty was sick when they picked it from the shelter. It wasn't until they got home that it started sneezing, and wasn't until even later that it started sneezing great big 2 foot long boogers out of its nose. But the shelter people gave them medicine, and it would be all better soon, and then I would get to meet it.

She failed to see my point. I had no intention of meeting it. I wanted it gone.

For nearly a week I had to listen to the sounds of

the little black furball running around the Younger Human's room. I had to put up with seeing the People slip into the room to play with it every day. I had to endure their refusal to touch me until after they had washed their hands after playing with it. I had to hear about how cute he was and how much energy he had.

Then one day the Woman set up The Cage. I had seen the cage before; when the Younger Human first brought me home, they had placed me in the cage so that I could meet Hank The Dog (who, by the time we left Evil Ohio, had been gone for over a year. He was a good dog, and I missed him for a long time even though I didn't exactly pay any attention to him while he was still alive. He was, after all, a dog, and being a dog, I had little use for him. But I missed him all the same.) After they had decided Hank would not eat me, I was allowed out of it to explore my new surroundings while someone kept Hank on a leash. When we demonstrated that we could keep our separate peace, they put the cage away and I thought it was gone.

But there it was, in the living room, with its door open, waiting.

And then the Woman brought out my blue Plastic Tomb, the one they had locked me in for the four days it took to get from Evil Ohio to the new place.

I wanted to run. I tried to run, but she grabbed me and put me in the tomb, and I was sure that I was about to be carried outside, put in the car, and taken to a new place to live. A place without my People or Younger Human.

I was being replaced, it had to be.

What, I wondered frantically, had I done so wrong

that the needed to replace me? Sure, I like to sing at the top of my lungs at 3 in the morning, but that's a *concert*, and they should *appreciate* it. And yeah, I like head butting the Woman's face to wake her up in the morning. And sometimes I like curling up my front paw like a tiny fist and punching her in the eye while she's asleep, but none of that is bad enough to get rid of me.

They weren't going to explain the why of any of it, I knew that. They were bigger and could do what they wanted, even if what they wanted was a new kitty at the expense of the old one.

A minute or so after I was locked into the Tomb, they brought it out. It was no bigger than a sneeze, just this wad of black fur with a tail and four little legs. They put it in the cage and closed the door, and then someone said, "Max, meet Buddah."

Buddah.

He didn't look like a Buddha to me. He didn't look nearly so wise. In fact, he looked more like Trouble.

That's what they should have named him. Trouble.

When I didn't hiss or spit or growl, the Woman opened the door of the Tomb and told me I could get out and get closer. On one hand, I felt a measure of relief because that probably meant I wasn't going anywhere. On the other...there was still this new kitty to deal with.

I sniffed at him; he sniffed back and didn't seem the least bit afraid of me. I told him to go away, but being so tiny I don't think he understood what I was saying. He just stood on his back legs and reached through the cage bars to touch me. I backed away, and then walked away, trying to look unimpressed.

After a while, they locked me in a bedroom to let

him run around the rest of the apartment. I fumed while I was in there, wondering what they could be thinking.

We thought you might want a play mate, someone had said.

NO I DO NOT!

A kitten can be fun.

No, no no no. NO.

We alternated; he had time running around the house, I had time running around the house. They wanted to gradually introduce us, as if taking baby steps would make me less wary of the little monster.

And then it happened.

I sneezed.

The People froze, and waited, hoping it was just one sneeze, perhaps from a little dust kicked up while stomping through the house.

And then I sneezed again.

And again.

I started coughing.

I stopped eating.

It was late on a Saturday, and the People said there was no place they could take me; that suited me just fine since I didn't want to be tossed away like a used tissue. They could put up with my sneezing and coughing; if sneezing and coughing meant getting rid of someone, I could have gotten rid of them all years ago.

The Man picked me up and said I felt hot.

The Woman said to keep Buddah away, make him stay in the Younger Human's room, don't stress out Max.

Well, it would have been nice if they'd done that all along, don't you think?

They fretted and fussed over me, pleading with me

to eat a little bit. Drink something. I wanted to; my tummy was growling, but my head was hurting and I couldn't stop coughing. The one time I tried to eat, I wound up barfing all over a pair of pants the Woman had set on top of her dresser.

That's when I knew it was bad. I threw up on her clean clothes, and she didn't mind. She didn't mind at all.

The next day the People got on the phone to tell some guy all about my sneezing and coughing and barfing. And as if it were interesting, he wanted to see me.

I did not want to see him, not at all.

In fact, I didn't want to see him so badly that when we got there, I growled at him. The Woman said I had met him before and he was a nice man, so be nice.

Then I remembered him: the stabby guy. The last time I had been to see him, he waited until I wasn't looking, and he stabbed me right in the butt. That was marginally better than what I had thought he was going to do; the People had originally told me they were taking me there to get shot. So maybe he didn't have his gun that day, but he found something nice and sharp to hurt me with.

So no, I did not want to be there. I already felt bad enough, but to be forced to see the bald guy at the stabby place? No, I wanted to go home.

Oh and he wanted to shove something up my butt, but when I refused to allow that he grabbed my ears and said Yes, he's got fever.

Then he really grabbed me and forced my mouth open. My throat was all clogged up with goop, he said. Well, I could have told him that. But he told the People that I was probably gagging on food, which is why I couldn't eat. And seeing as how the little black monster had been sick, he gave them the same medicine the shelter people had given them.

The Woman told me it should make me feel better in a couple of days.

A couple of days later I was sicker than before, suffering explosions from both ends. It was tiring, and it was humiliating, having the People watch me in the litter box, commenting on my deposits therein.

And they took me back to see the bald guy at the stabby place. I was so tired that I couldn't stop him from doing things to me, things I'd rather not talk about. But he said to stop giving me the medicine since that was probably what caused the explosions from my hind quarters, and then said something that caused fear to run in sheets of electric tingles right through the tip of my tail.

"We should probably steal all his blood and look at it."

Ok, that's not a direct quote, but that's what he meant, and he did it! He STABBED me again and drained off a good part of my blood, and I'm pretty sure I needed that! Worse, he didn't give it back when he was done looking at it. *And* he took something else to stab me with, only he shoved a bunch of water under my skin, the penalty for not being able to drink.

Look, there should be no rules against not drinking. If a kitty does not feel like drinking, then leave him alone! What good does shoving water under his skin do when its his MOUTH that's thirsty? Sheesh.

I was so annoyed, that I pooped all over the place. That nice shiny table they make a kitty sit on in the stabby place—I pooped all over that. I mean, I *really* pooped.

The Woman took me back home, and I retreated to a safe, dark place: her closet. I could rest in there and it was quiet, and all I really wanted was to be alone. And if I was in there, they could close the bedroom door and let that little crackhead kitty run around.

He needs to run around, she explained to me.

At that point, I didn't care.

I didn't care about anything.

Not about food.

Not about treats.

Not about that other kitty.

I stopped caring, and the People could see that, and the Woman admitted she was very scared. She sat on the floor just outside the closet and told me there were lots of people and kitties all over the world pulling for me to get better. They knew all about me and were saying prayers for me, sending me good thoughts and 52 kinds of Get-Well-Max-Mojo. I *had* to get better.

It's not as if I was trying to die. I wanted to get better more than anyone else, if for no other reason than I had to lay the smackdown on that little black monster and let him know who the boss of the house really was.

I was hungry, so very hungry. I wanted to eat because a little voice in my head said if I did, I would feel lots better. The People kept offering me my favorite things, like shrimp and tuna water. The Woman even went to the store and bought some People baby food, because the bald guy said sometimes sick kitties with eat baby food. At least it wasn't hamburger and rice.

(When Hank the dog was sick and stopped eating, the Woman saw on TV that some old dogs and sick dogs who didn't like their own food anymore would eat hamburger and rice. So every day she made up a bunch of hamburger and rice. She cooked for him for weeks, even when she wouldn't cook food for the Man. Hank ate it, happily, for a couple of weeks. When he didn't seem to have the energy to eat on his own, the People put chunks of food on a fork and hand fed him. I watched them do this and thought they were a little nuts, especially when they had a dinner for themselves and made up a whole plate for him, but the Woman said Hank could have whatever he wanted as long as he would eat. They gave him his favorite food one dinner time, steak, and he was happy as a fly on a big pile of Hank poop, but the next day he went to the Rainbow Bridge, so you can see why I was glad it wasn't hamburger and rice that the Woman cooked for me, because that would have meant this was all a Really Big Bad.)

The baby food smelled really tasty, and I wanted it, but there was something inside me that wouldn't let me eat. I knew if I started to eat I'd feel better, but I couldn't figure that out. How do I start eating again? They were sticking this awful brown goo into my mouth because it had lots of calories and nutrition, but it made me gag worse. They gave me chunks of a medicine that was supposed to make my appetite big, but it was already big, I was really hungry, but I just couldn't figure out how to start.

Then one day after I had been sick for a week or so, after a couple trips to the stabby place so they could shove water under my skin again, and when the Woman really was worried that I was going to follow Hank to the Rainbow Bridge, I smelled chicken. So I went into the kitchen, and the Woman was getting ready to make chicken salad.

I couldn't even meow I was so tired and sick, so I bumped my head on her leg, and when she looked down she asked, "Do you want a bite?"

I thought I might, but I couldn't say so. I just sat there, looking as pathetic as I felt, but she understood. She grabbed her bowl of shredded chicken and sat in the floor, where she put a tiny piece out for me.

I licked it. That was the best start I could make, I licked it.

I heard the Man's voice, but the Woman turned and whispered just loud enough for me to hear, "Don't come in. He's trying to eat and I don't want you to distract him."

So he stopped right where he was and didn't move.

I nibbled at the chicken, I licked and nibbled, and as little pieces made it down my throat the Woman put more in front of me. It was a steady stream of tiny chicken chunks, she kept sticking them there, hoping momentum would get some real food into me.

Pretty soon I was just too tired, but she scratched behind my ears and said, "Good job!" as if I was a little human child, and normally that would have annoyed me, but she was right. I did a good job with that chicken. I heard her tell the Man I had probably eaten almost a full tablespoon, and that was a good start.

The next day I ate a little more. The man gave me tuna water, with tiny flecks of tuna in it. I ate a little, and took a nap. I didn't eat much the rest of that day because I was wiped out, but the next morning my stomach woke me up, and I knew.

I could eat if they put food in front of me.

I still didn't feel very good—I had awful tummy

pains and a royal headache—but I could eat. So the Woman offered me some Stinky Goodness, and I ate it. I ate it all.

The worst of it, I was sure, had to be over. I was not going to run off to the Bridge to see Hank, and I was going to be able to lay the smackdown on the little crackhead soon. And no more bald guy.

I thought.

They took me back to the bald guy at the stabby place; I was sure they just wanted to show me off, tell him what a good job I'd done, eating the chicken and getting myself all better. He was appropriately impressed, but I didn't let him touch me. Heck no.

There was bad news, he said. "His blood work shows he has pancreatitis."

I'm going to die!

I was sure of it.

All that hard work getting better and I was going to die!

The Woman did not seem upset enough, not for my taste. So I started to climb her like a tree, got onto her shoulder, and as I slid down her arm, I pooped on her.

I am the Poop-At-Will King, after all.

I pooped so thoroughly and so well that people in the waiting room were gagging. The Woman's eyes watered, but all she did was take the wet towel the bald guy offered and cleaned her arm off. He said she could use their shower thingy, but she said no, she would shower at home. I think she just didn't want to get naked there, but I know she didn't like smelling that bad. And she *really* smelled bad after that.

We're going to shove these little chunks down his throat, the bald guy told her. Two times every day for 2 weeks, shove half a chunk down his throat. When he's good and ticked off, stop. We'll let him go two weeks and he'll think it's all over, but then you need to do it again. Chunks twice a day for two weeks.

Yep, that's what he said. It was all "Oh, let's RE-ALLY tick off the kitty! It will be so much fun!"

But then I heard something else. He intimated that I'd probably been born with this problem, which can be fatal, and if I hadn't gotten sick…who knows? He could have felt bad off and on and you just never knew about it.

She thought I was just a snarky kitty, not that I had tummy aches.

Then she asked him for how long would I have to swallow these chunks for two out of ever four weeks.

Forever.

For. Ev. Er.

When we got home I was not a happy kitty. I did not want to see the little black monster, I did not want to play with him. I wanted to sit on him and make him cry. I was still a little sick, though, so they didn't let us be alone together long enough for me to do anything to him.

And then it hit me as I watched him run at full tilt up and down the hall like someone had stuck a firecracker to his tail.

If he hadn't shown up when he did, shooting those 2 foot long boogers out of his nose, the People might have never found out that there was something wrong inside me that might have eventually killed me. I would have had these huge tummy aches and they would have assumed it was just me being me, all mean and snarky and stuff.

Buddah ran up and jumped on me, his paws grabbing for my head as if he were trying to hug me, not rip my head off.

"I will never really like you," I told him. "That's just the way it is. But I'll put up with you, and sometimes I'll play with you, because you're just a baby and babies need to be played with. But I don't have to like you, not at all."

"That's ok," he squealed, biting my ear. "You're my big brother. Someday you'll love me. You don't ever have to *like* me."

Holy…

Dang it.

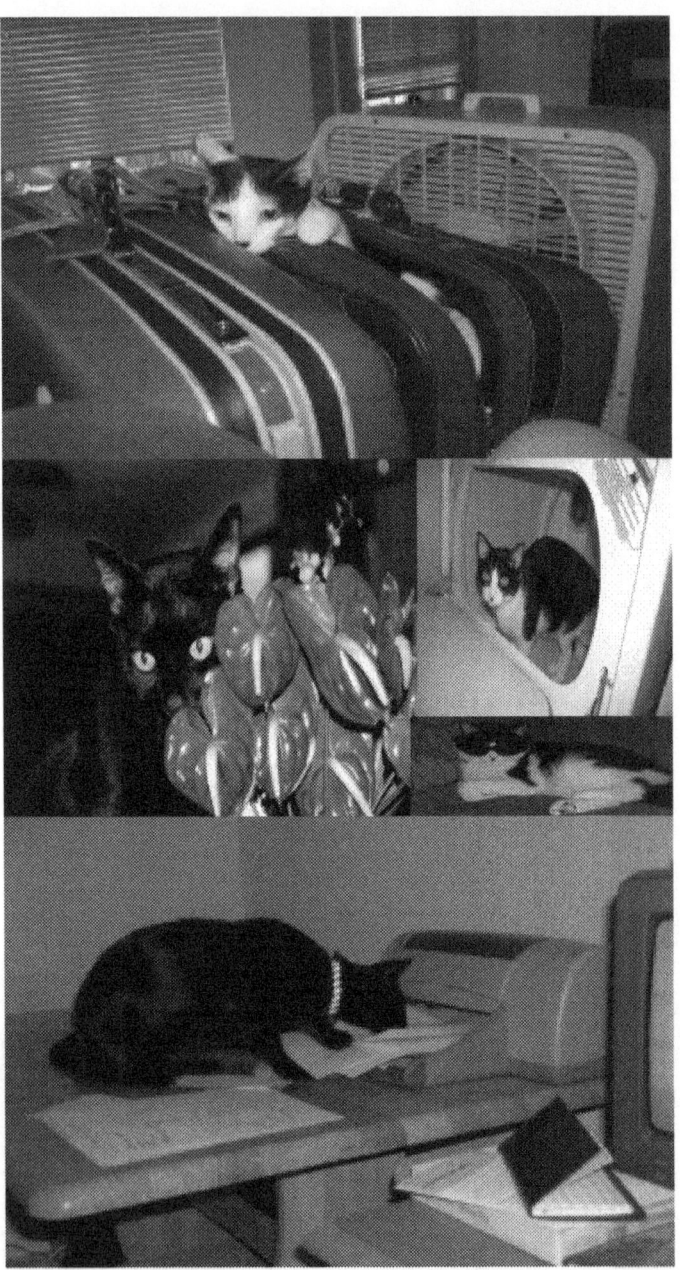

Last page.
You can close the book now.
Contemplate on what you learned.
Or don't close the book.
Sit and look at my picture.
Enjoy the wonder that is me.
You deserve that much.

~Max, aka Psychokitty

Really.... Book's done.

Go on now.

Go outside and get some fresh air.

Really... you could use some fresh air.

Oh, you're not going to, are you?

I see how it is, you with your People ways.

Stay inside. See if I care.

Go feed the kitty. The kitty wants crunchy treats.

And thank you for buying this book. Some kitty somewhere might just get a can of Stinky Goodness tonight
because you did. A kitty might live another day, a chance
to find a Forever Home. Go hug your kitty now, and
give him some crunchy treats...

www.ingramcontent.com/pod-product-compliance
Lightning Source LLC
Chambersburg PA
CBHW052133170626
46812CB00004B/1393